What readers are saying about

Home Is Where The Fish Are

Not only the characters, but the issues faced by intrepid Alaskans are portrayed spot on.

If you wish to gain some insight into life in small town Alaska while being delightfully entertained this becomes a must read.

Fish stories and local gossip are vehicles for the real story - an insightful look at love's power - and its limits - through the years. The stories of the town's residents twine together to show you the fabric of small town Alaska.
Recommended for those interested in Alaska, fishing, and those who love a good story.

This multi-faceted little gem invites the reader to witness a terrible beauty of both nature and the human heart. If this were not enough, she also educates us on the fishing industry and national politics surrounding it. Well done!

She captures the individuality of the people who choose to live in this isolated region while reminding us that human frailty is universal. And all that with a creative turn of phrase and a subtle sense of humor.

HOME IS WHERE THE FISH ARE

Christi Slaven

Harold, Emily, and Syd are real. Harold and Emily were gone by the time I was ready to make this book public. Syd, however, gave it his full support and blessing.

All other characters in this story are creations of my imagination.

Really.

No matter what you think.

Others:

Earl Dahlberg, who is married to Betty, who is cousin to

Carla Marten, who is married to Jim and is niece to

Dwayne Dickson, who is married to Myra.

Sandy Bergren, who is married to Belle and chair of the board that hired

Neil Esterhaus, who is older brother to

Steve Esterhaus, who has hired

Holli Franklin to deckhand for him.

Arlen Pinkstad, who is editor of the local weekly and for whom

Darlene Cartwright works. Darlene is married to Ray.

Gabriella Hanson, Rudy Valente, retired fishermen

Mack Harrison, Warren Olsen, Deaf Tony, working fishermen

Fishing Vessel Types

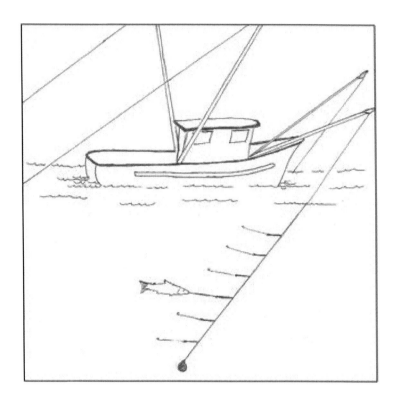

Wildly oversimplified Troller

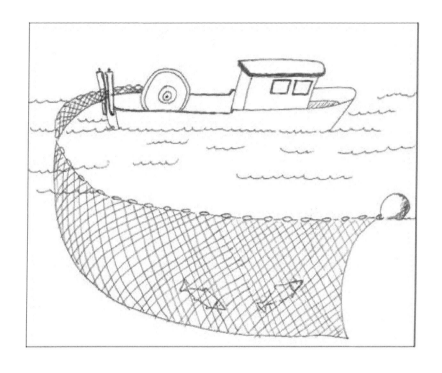

Vastly oversimplified Gillnetter

Ridiculously oversimplified Longliner

Earl hunched over the steel salmon gaff and sharpening file in his lap and tried to let her words roll over him. He knew the litany by heart, each syllable a drumbeat of accusation.

"Years of puking my guts out over the rail, busting my knuckles, yelled at, cussed at, being treated like a two-bit, greenhorn deckhand and biting my tongue. And where did my share of the profits go, Earl? Where did my vacations to Mexico go? My diamond earrings? My Buick? Just a friggin' Buick, Earl! Not a Town Car, not a Coup DeVille, just a lousy Buick. I'll tell you where it went. It all went into the business. Everything went into the business. I bought and paid for every stinking pound of that quota with blisters and a sore back and these bags under my eyes. I deserve it and more," she spat. "I deserve your soul on a plate."

"For Chrissake," he said, dropping the gaff and file on the floor as he threw his hands in the air. "I worked, too. I worked hard."

Her shoulders sagged and she shook her head.

"I know it, Earl. You worked, I worked, we worked, the kids worked." She looked down at her hands and flexed the broken knuckle that had healed so crookedly, traced the scar that ran the length of her thumb. She pressed her sandpaper palms together and brought them up to her chin. Her eyes brailled his face for some glimmer of understanding. His eyes searched hers for some crumb of a clue.

"I had dreams, Earl."

He snorted and threw her words back in a sing song whine, "I had dreams, Earl." He was going to say how he had dreams too, how he wanted to get some things paid off, maybe even get far enough ahead so the two of them could take a day off now and then. But before he could, an animal growl rattled out of her throat.

"You think it's funny?"

Her eyes narrowed to blazing slits. He watched her inflate before him like an angry cat. Her back arched as she rose off the couch and her shoulders unfurled like raptor wings. The hair stood up all over her head.

"You think it's funny!" she screamed.

Earl stood too, stumbling slightly. "No, I don't. Now just calm down."

Suddenly the newly sharpened gaff was in her hand and he was backing toward the nearest door. She gripped the hardwood club with both hands and swung the end with the glistening five inch hook in it seriously close to his ear. He lunged through the opening.

"Betty, I was just kidding," he hollered as he paused on the porch.

"Honey?" He turned and took the steps two at a time.

She walked slowly down the stairs, never taking her eyes off him. He backed up, stumbling over coils of crab line in the yard. Then he felt a head high stack of pots behind him.

"Betty?"

She swung hard and he ducked. The steel mesh of the pot twanged as it absorbed the blow, and the gaff hook tangled for a second in the wire. He dodged behind the stack.

"Dwayne? Dwayne, come here. Quick!"

Dwayne put the paper down and sauntered toward the kitchen. Myra stood at the sink holding the curtain aside. She waved him over impatiently.

"She's chasing after him with a gaff hook."

12

He glanced out the window. "Yeanh."

"Dwayne, do something!"

He watched the deadly game of tag next door. Earl ducked and dodged between stacks of crab pots while Betty swung and staggered after him. Earl shouted and waved his arms. Betty was mute and furious.

"Looks like they're working it out," he said.

Myra flinched.

"That was close. Stop her, Dwayne."

"You want me to put myself between him and that steel gaff? I don't think so."

He turned away and walked back toward the living room.

"Aren't you going to do anything at all?" she called after him.

"Yeanh. I'm going to finish the paper. You let me know how it turns out."

Myra dropped the curtain and glared after him. In one last furtive peek, she saw Betty chase Earl around the corner of the house. Dwayne watched her over the top of the paper as she sat down beside him. She ignored him with studied silence.

"I'm not a busybody," she insisted at last. "I just didn't want to see him killed."

"If you didn't want to see it, you shouldn't have been peeking out the kitchen window." He returned to the classifieds.

"Honestly," she grumbled.

A slamming door and a loud metallic crash jarred them both.

"Hood of the truck, I'd guess," said Dwayne without looking up.

Shattering glass.

"Mmm, Windshield, probably."

Spun gravel and the screech of tires on asphalt.

Myra craned her neck to watch as Earl sped by the living room window. Broken glass flew off the hood and peppered both sides of the street. She leaned back and picked up her needlepoint. They sat

13

in silence for several minutes, with only the rasp of her wool through canvas and the rustle of his paper.

"You're right," she finally said with a sigh. "Nothing exciting ever happens around here."

Dwayne eyed her again over the rims of his reading glasses, "Depends on what excites you, I guess."

Myra jerked the yarn as tight as her thin frown and severed the air with one silver snap of the scissors.

Legitimate use for a salmon gaff hook.

"And now for the local weather; rain changing to showers this afternoon. So what else is new, eh? Rain changing to showers, showers changing to rain, and sometimes, just to spice things up, a little sleet or hail thrown in. Maybe if we brought back human sacrifice, the weather gods might be a little nicer to us, do you think? Ah well, it keeps the bugs down and the tourists away. Now let's have a look at the Birthday Book for this week coming up. Sunday, April 14th, Happy Birthday to Chris Lofton." There were several seconds of dead air before Harold hollered, not to his radio audience, "Hey, I thought he was dead." He lifted one earphone and waited for a reply.

Emily's exasperated squawk came from deep within the record stacks. "He is dead. He died last August. Had a heart attack out on his boat."

"Why's his name still in here then?"

"I can't do everything, Harold. Cross it out and get on with it, for pity sake!"

Harold carefully drew a line through Chris's name and replaced his earphone.

"Sorry, about that, folks. When you get to be my age, it's hard to keep track of all the people passing to the Great Beyond. Dropping like a bunch of damned flies. Why, I check the notices on the post office door every time I come to town just to make sure I'm not supposed to be at my own funeral. Let me see, where were we?"

Emily was a long time fixture at the local radio station--some thought too long--and one of the few who actually got paid. Harold was a long retired, long time volunteer DJ. He violated broadcast etiquette so often that the FM station on this damp island in southeast

16

Alaska regularly preceded his Saturday morning program with a disclaimer. Even Harold didn't usually editorialize on the Birthday Book, but sometimes things just had to be set straight.

"Let's see, also on April 14th, Carolee Harris and Lionel Smith. Monday, April 15th, Happy Birthday to Betty Dahlberg."

Harold ripped the earphones from his head again. He twisted his arthritic neck toward the next room.

"Dagone it, Emily, is it Betty Dahlberg or is it Betty Esterhaus?"

His snappish query was faint but clearly audible as was Emily's reply.

"Neil Esterhaus, you mean? Nah, she hasn't married Neil. But she sure as heck did move Earl out."

"Hummmpf," mumbled Harold as he replaced the headset. "Oh, well, none of my business. Maybe he's better off. Maybe they're both better off. Where was I? Here we are. Also on Monday, Glen Fortenau, Gladys Barton and Darlene Cartwright. Tuesday, April 16th, Darrel McCullough. Wednesday, April 17th, Lyle Corbett and Holli Franklin, and on the 18th, a very Happy Anniversary goes out to Jim and Carla Marten. April 19th..."

"If we make it to Thursday," thought Carla as she flung Jim's underwear in the washer. She splashed undiluted bleach on top, slammed the lid down, and gave the start knob a vicious twist. She punched the radio off and jerked the unsuspecting vacuum cleaner from its hiding place, but a timid knock on the door postponed the punishment the carpet was about to receive. Earl Dahlberg slumped against the doorjamb.

Carla felt seismic tension between the two halves of her face, the eyes and brow in a cramped downward curve and the mouth struggling upward into a neighborly welcome.

"Jim home?" Earl asked without moving.

"No, sorry, Earl. They left this morning for a couple of days," she answered. "Green crew..." *peroxide blonde is more like it...* "He

17

wanted to try some bait sets for practice. Is there something I can help you with?"

"Nah, I just...it's just...I..."

"Come on in," she said, summoning what compassion she could. "Coffee's still hot."

Earl heelshucked his rubber boots inside the door and, not finding an empty hook to hang it on, carried his greasy baseball cap with him. His back and knees, bent and bowed and from years on the ocean, made him shorter than Carla by a head.

"Sit down, Earl. I'll be right back."

She dumped two loads of sugar into a mug and filled it with the second cup of coffee Jim hadn't had time for. *Gotta get down to the boat,* he had said, *crew's waiting for me.*

"Crew's waiting for me," mimicked Carla bitterly. She pulled a deep breath and tipped her head back, straightening her tall frame into a prideful stance. "Fake it til you make it," she murmured to herself. She picked up Earl's coffee and her lukewarm tea and walked back into the living room. Earl had alighted on her new taupe loveseat. He was turning his cap around and around in his hands. As she passed him his cup, he hung the cap on his knee. She waited.

"Betty," he began.

Carla nodded. She knew where he was going and knew he had to get there by himself. Earl dropped his head and heaved a sigh. She could see his bald spot like a shiny egg in a nest of coarse straw and twigs. He carried the smell of diesel fumes and old rubber that meant he was sleeping on the boat.

He looked up and drew a deep breath.

"You and Jim have been our friends for a long time."

Carla nodded again.

"You especially," he said brightening. "I remember our first day in first grade."

18

"You mean that morning recess when I was sitting on your chest ready to punch you in the face?"

Earl dipped his head, still a little embarrassed and they smiled easily across the comfort of years.

"It was the last time I ever pulled a punch in a fight, you know," she said.

"I know it and I'm still grateful."

He set his cup on the glass end table, slopping only a little onto the gleaming surface. He picked up his hat again and examined the full circle of the sweatband. When he looked up, his eyes were brimming with tears.

"Betty," he said again. "She's taking my halibut quota."

"What?" Carla leaned forward in her chair.

"She's taking my IFQs," he repeated. He shook his head from side to side like a dog trying to shake water but too dazed to do more than drip. Carla felt as though the ground had shifted beneath her. Her dark brows pulled together and, as she tilted her head away from Earl, she kept her eyes focused sharply on his face.

"You two have argued," she paused, considering, "from time to time. Every couple does. But you've always patched things up."

"Not this time." He shook his head again. "She says she's gonna sell my halibut poundage to the highest bidder and buy herself all the things I never did."

Carla closed her eyes, tried to think back to the year the government had divided up the halibut catch among the participating fishermen. As bookkeeper and tax consultant for the whole family, she had been in charge of transferring Earl's poundage into Betty's name and Jim's into hers so that the two men could buy the rights to harvest more poundage from other fishermen.

"How much quota did we put in Betty's name?"

"Thirty two thousand pounds almost. I went ahead and bought those two smaller blocks, but together they don't come close to the one block of quota shares she's got. This is gonna break me, Carla. She got me by the short hairs now."

Carla cupped her chin in her hand and tapped one blood red fingernail against her cheek as she stared at the wall just above Earl's lolling head. Her eyes squinted into the distance for an instant then focused once more on the miserable man grinding grease stains into her sofa.

She drew a deep breath, exhaled, then said, not without feeling, "I don't think there's anything you can do, Earl. As far as the law's concerned, they're hers and she can do whatever she wants with them."

"She's really got me by the balls," he whined.

"Yes." Carla nodded her head several times. "Yes, she does."

"You'll talk to her, won't you? I mean, you're family. She'll listen to you."

"What do you want me to say, Earl?"

"Explain to her how it ain't right, how you can't just take everything a man's worked for and just, well, just take it. You can't. You rip a man's guts out."

"Yes," she said slowly, the nodding of her head growing stronger, "I definitely need to talk to her."

"Somebody needs to talk sense to her. She's acting like a damned fool with that Neil Esterhaus. You remember him. I never did like him. Never could stand him. I can't for the life of me understand why she wants to have anything to do with him."

Splotches of color rose above Earl's bunched collar and into the shrubbery of several days' stubble. He stiffened, squeezing his hat into a tight ball. Carla nodded calmly and watched him collapse again like a sail gone slack.

"I don't know what to do. You can see she's really got me by the...well, she really does."

"Yes, I see she does. I'll talk to her. Soon."

20

He stood, tugging the wrinkled cap onto his shaggy head. A gray smear stayed behind on the cushion.

"You're the best, Carla."

She showed Earl out and emptied his untouched coffee down the sink. She bent to reach Windex and the upholstery cleaner, then paused. She leaned against the counter and stared down the drain. She tapped an enameled nail against the stainless steel rim. Her dark eyes grew dangerously darker and narrowed to angry slits. Her lips drew tight. At last she struck the counter with the flat of both hands.

"Earl, you'd better by God drag those balls over, and make room for Jim, 'cause here comes the vise!"

Neil Esterhaus had come home trailing three failed marriages behind, paste jewels shattered on the pavements of various West Coast cities. Neil was the oldest of the Esterhaus boys, slight and vaguely red headed. The fiction that made him so much smaller than his stocky blond brothers was that he was born nearly two months prematurely. In fact, Helena Esterhaus had been almost six weeks pregnant when Berle returned from a stint on a Bering Sea crabber.

Virginal at marriage, her huge Norwegian husband had frightened her stiff and for three years their marriage had been a trial for them both. One winter, while Berle was beating the ice off the superstructure of a crab boat in screaming twenty below gales, the local Arts Council had sponsored a performance by a traveling theater troupe from San Francisco.

One young man with a Frisco tan and a dancer's legs had drawn Helena to him like a magnet. Singly they abandoned the post performance coffee and krumkake and met outside the gymnasium doors. He shivered in the light snowfall. Steam rose from her dampening hair. She led him through the back door of her own home. The smells of her life and Berle's greeted her there, the wool and rubber of Berle's work clothes hanging by the back door and the piercing scent of cedar from the stack by the living room stove. The smell of her small supper still hung in the white enameled kitchen. Then the scent of his cologne curled around her from behind. They made love in the middle of the darkened living room, the rough wool rug biting deep into her back.

She raced toward him propelled by the cresting wave of three years' hunger. He devoured her with the practiced care of a professional glutton, all the same grateful for the meal.

Berle's mother, Grace, and Aunt Gloria had comforted Helena all through the pregnancy, patted her shoulder kindly and said they, too, had experienced unpredictable fits of crying and it would pass. Berle had said little as Berle was wont to do, and said only, "Hot damn!" when their marriage bed began to rock with a new sort of Lutheran determination. In fact, he blamed their unbound enthusiasm for Neil's early arrival.

Three more boys had tumbled out after Neil. Carl, Sven, and finally, Steve. These blond, big boned boys were rough timber Berle could build with but Neil was slick. Claiming a professional destiny, he slid out of town right after high school, sucked up four years of his father's fish money, and announced he never intended to return. But the detritus of his life had piled too high and finally pushed him back to a place of no less painful, but somewhat more eroded memories.

By now the meeting in Neil's office had already dragged well into its second hour. Sandy's eyes traced the juncture of the walls and ceiling before him back and forth, wondering to himself how this Esterhaus guy could work in here day after day not even knowing what the weather was. Sandy always felt best outside and his handsome, weathered face attested to that. The creases around his eyes fanned mostly upward, also testimony to the satisfaction he felt in his career and marriage. These agonizing, endless meetings were the only thing that drug those smile lines down

This guy talked way too fast and used a string of hundred dollar words when a two bit adjective would serve just as well. And though Sandy knew far more than Neil about the past and present of the business and the town in general, he was unsure about the future Neil was proposing. It was discomforting in his position as chairman of the board.

When he had married gentle Belle, he hadn't realized he was marrying the family's marine hardware business as well. Belle's brother-in-law, husband to her older sister, had been comfortable at the head of this table. When he had died suddenly two years ago, the store had already signed on with a national hardware franchise and was irrevocably committed to a new, larger site above town. The old store down by the docks with its oiled wood floors and narrow aisles became a repository for a growing array of souvenir sweatshirts and other tourist kitsch. The new store had looked like a smart move at the time. The town was growing, fish populations were strong, prices were up, the IFQ program was brand new and had the support of the biggest fish processing plant in town.

Sandy also sat on that board of directors, a position inherited from his own father, and had squirmed uneasily with management's decision to back the program. In granting the rights to a certain percentage of the yearly catch--an Individual Fisherman's Quota based on past participation--the program destroyed the competition that these stubbornly independent men thrived on.

"Might as well be pickin' potatoes," his father had grumbled.

Sandy had done all right, being at the height of his career. He had, in fact, become an instant millionaire because the rights to his quota were worth in the beginning six, then fourteen, and now nearly twenty dollars per pound to any fisherman looking to get into or expand his share of the fishery. And now this guy, this slick haired guy with the gattling gun mouth, this Esterhaus, so unlike the other Esterhaus brothers was telling him--he thought he was telling him--that IFQs were destroying Belle's father's business.

True, profits had been sliding ever since the business had moved into its new quarters. Interest, insurance, inflation were all nibbling at the bottom line. They had been forced to curtail credit at the store from a whole season to a month and then to only ten days. But Esterhaus, like an increasing number of Main Street moguls chose to lay the blame on IFQs. Sandy figured it was mostly greed, arrogance, greed, incompetence, greed, short sightedness, plain old stupidity, and greed that drove infuriated customers away, but it was much easier to point hasty fingers at IFQs than to look in the mirror.

The room had grown silent around him. He furrowed his brow to simulate thought. He wanted the Dick and Jane version, not the Oxford unabridged and he knew how to get it. Knowing Esterhaus saw as much invitation in a comma as most people saw in a period and an if-you-please, he said, "So what you're saying is..."

Neil perched on the edge of the table and held up four fingers. Pressing the first down, he said, "One, fewer guys are gearing up. Used to be everybody and his fourth grade teacher fished halibut.

Two, the guys who are gearing up are buying less gear because A, they're not laying a carpet of hooks out there in a 24 hour opening and losing half of it and B, it's so much less competitive that guys are taking their time and fishing 50 skates again and again instead of 200 skates all at once.

Three, they're not pressured by a single make or break opening into buying everything they need locally. They have time to order it out of Seattle. If they don't make it out today, they leave for the grounds when they're ready tomorrow or next week.

Four, a more leisurely pace means fewer deckhands, fewer dollars being spread around town, and fewer dollars to the general hardware section of the store.

And five, the big one," he said, raising his thumb and folding it back down, "these guys are selling to a fresh market almost year round. Places like Juneau and Sitka with lots of daily jet service are offering higher prices and guys just aren't bringing their catch back here to Podunkville. Again fewer dollars to us."

Sandy nodded. He knew the cannery was seeing smaller profits, but he suspected mismanagement at the highest levels, rather than IFQs. He offered Esterhaus another invitation to expound.

"So what you're proposing is..."

"Dump the IFQ program."

Sandy threw up his hands. "Neil, that's been through the courts twice and failed both times. There's too many guys have invested too much in buying IFQs to just chuck it. You know your brother Steve mortgaged everything he owns to buy halibut IFQs. What about him?"

Neil smiled blandly.

"I don't propose throwing out the whole program tomorrow. This company has reserves to sit out a number of lean years. I do propose getting behind some amendments to the program that will allow more fishermen--the smaller, strictly local operations the store depends on-- allowing them to participate."

Sandy rubbed his forehead with one hand and clenched the arm of the chair with the other. He tried to breathe deeply but found no air in Neil's windowless office.

He gazed down at his right shoe, a creased and comfortable deck slipper with a well worn heel. He rolled his foot and saw saltwater stains high on the instep. Iridescent herring scales clung to the sole. He glanced at Neil's oxblood wingtip dangling at the end of an unmuscled leg.

"What amendments, Neil?"

Neil oozed from the table and paced back and forth in front of the assembled board.

"Fishermen want to catch fish."

Sandy didn't need it simplified to this degree and felt his blood pressure rise ten points with every declarative sentence.

"We want the IFQs to stay in the hands of small operators."

He knew Neil had college degrees and had managed several businesses and even a political campaign, though this last was no recommendation in Sandy's eyes. The business was in trouble. He would grit his teeth and hear the man out.

26

"There are several options." He raised those bony fingers in front of their faces again. "We can ask that IFQs be made nontransferable, so that one fisherman cannot sell them to another."

Sandy shot out of his chair. Several hundred thousand dollars had just vanished from his retirement fund.

"No way!" he roared.

Neil closed his eyes and raised his hands calmly. Oil seemed to descend into the room.

"OR," he said, "only transferable for those to whom they were initially issued."

Sandy fell back into his chair and gripped the leather arms again until his knuckles turned white. Though his future seemed secure once more, his head was still pounding furiously. Neil went on.

"I've read the entire text of the regulations and the language makes it quite clear that the intent was to retain the character of the original fleet, that is, small operators, not large corporations, and local sales, not a mass migration to major transportation hubs. I think we can persuade the federal boys to smile on this amendment. If the quota shares revert back to the feds when a fisherman retires or dies, the feds will get to decide how to divvy them back up. They'll like that, I'm sure. And I'm also sure we can make a case for keeping the shares in communities like ours where they belong."

Neil smiled greasily, looking at everyone but Sandy. The others nodded. Some even smiled back. Sandy's mouth grew hard and his eyes narrowed.

"What about people like Stevie, who bought their shares? What about guys who took the risk, invested every penny they had, and worked like the devil to build a business? What about them?"

Neil shrugged blandly. "Some people will have to adjust." He shrugged again. "There will no doubt be some losers, but the important thing is, this business will survive and even thrive again. Profits and stockholder dividends will be fat."

"He's your brother, Neil"

"But I'm not his keeper, am I?"

"I move we adopt Mr. Esterhaus' plan," said Dorrie King quickly. Dorrie was Belle's second cousin, the customary tag for almost any obscure or convoluted relationship in town. Having run off two husbands with her drinking before becoming sanctimoniously sober, she lived almost entirely on dividends from the store.

"I second," said Danny Walden, Sandy's own nephew. Danny also fished, but never quite hard enough to make a profit. He, too, depended heavily on his dividends.

It devolved to Sandy to call for a vote. He looked around the room and realized how far from the working heart of this town his board members were. Aside from Danny, he was the only person in the room who knew what to do with the shackles, fids, snubbers, Canadians, bear traps, turnbuckles, lead lines, weed lines, buoys, float backs, hootchies, hog rings, plungers, plugs, and picks they sold in the building below.

He straightened in a futile search for another breath of air.

"Those in favor?" he asked.

"Aye," came the chorus.

"Those opposed?" The room was ebulliently silent.

"Motion passes." He turned to Neil, who gave the room a small bow.

"All right then," said Neil and he nodded in turn to each board member as he or she rose to go. When Sandy reached the door, Neil's voice stopped him.

"I'll be expecting your help in getting the processors behind these proposals. We need their muscle."

Sandy turned without raising his head. He only cocked it dangerously to one side.

"You know I don't like this idea, Neil."

Neil stopped stacking papers and smiled silkily.

28

"I know you'll do what's best for the business."

"Whose business?" Sandy's glare slid off Neil like rain off a rubber boot. He closed the door with ominous care. He needed coffee. He needed to talk to Belle. And he desperately needed some real air.

Arlen Pinkstad was a molder of minds, a sculptor of public opinion. He liked to see himself as a beacon of reason, but knew his mind worked far more slowly than his nimble fingers and that the taunting cursor on his computer screen along with looming deadlines forced him to simply rephrase the opinions he heard on his frequent breaks to the coffee shop or hurried trips to the post office.

There was so little printable news on the island that this newspaper, like so many others, stayed afloat by featuring large, clippable photographs of Youth Soccer, Students of the Month, Eagle Scout ceremonies, local Eastern Stars hosting visiting Eastern Stars, engagement announcements, and obituaries.

His arched fingers tapped the keyboard impatiently. His balding head atop an impossibly long neck drooped like a human question mark over the computer. Here finally with this IFQ thing was an issue he could come down on one side or the other of. He could lead his people to the high road, the lofty moral ground, if only he could discern in precisely which direction that ground lay.

EDITORIAL stood in bold letters at the top of his composing screen. *by Arlen Pinkstad* trailed in more modest italics. His fingers tapped the keyboard in frustration again and he was forced to backspace through a series of nonsense letters. He looked up at the clock.

"Darlene," he shouted, pushing back from his desk and, snagging his coat from a nearby chair, "you've got the phone. I'm going out for a cup of coffee."

He was already gone when Darlene sauntered out from the printing room wiping her hands on a cotton rag. She wandered over to Arlen's desk and glanced at the screen.

"Yeah, right. Coffee, my ass." Then she refilled her own cup from the office machine and wandered back to the presses, balancing her weight on one enormous hip then the other. She upped the volume on the radio since Arlen was gone and went back to oiling the drums.

"...two dogs have lost their owners. One is a young poodle type dog with no collar and the other is a husky mix with an apparent attitude about poodles. The police request that the owners pick up their dogs as soon as possible.

And one more announcement here. This is from Syd. Will whoever was in charge of the seafood chowder for the Troll King and Visqueen Ball last fall please contact Syd Wright at the high school? He'd like to borrow the cauldron for the senior play.

Now, a quick look in the Birthday Book for today. Glen Fortenau...uhm, I think he might have moved back to Michigan. Yes, I'm sure he did, because he borrowed a book from me and I never got it back. Well, I doubt he's listening, but Happy Birthday, Glen, and consider the book a gift. Who else? Uhm, Gladys Barton and Darlene Cartwright. Happy Birthday, all!"

"Yeah," mumbled Darlene as she lowered herself to the floor to reach the lowest grease zerks, "Happy Birthday to me."

"Are you really going to sell them or are you just messing with Earl?"

Carla stood at the kitchen window. She tucked the phone under her jaw and plucked yellowing leaves from the philodendron spilling across the sill.

"Hell, yes, I'm gonna sell them! Well, probably I am. Maybe. I don't know. I haven't made up my mind for sure. All I know is I'm so mad at him I could spit."

"What'd he do?"

"Same as he always does. Nothing. I spill my guts. I lay it all out and he makes fun of me. LAUGHS at me! Son of a bitch. I've had it."

"I don't blame you."

"If I leave it up to him, nothing will ever change. And why should it? He's got everything he wants."

"Well, you've certainly got his attention now."

"Twenty six years and I've finally got his attention for five minutes. That's not bad."

Carla laughed. "That's more than most women ever get," and she could hear a smile on the other end of the line. She pictured her cousin as the girl whose smile used to light up a room. It was a smile that had grown grudging with the years, just as her once dark hair had become gray as dust and her slim waist had thickened to sausage sameness. Carla had fared a little better. Naturally slimmer, she had also fought the years with diets, exercise and the skillfully subtle application of make up and hair color.

"Something else has his attention, too. He's pretty upset about all the time you've been spending with Neil. Should he be?"

"Neil?" Carla could tell by the surprise in her voice that the thought was a new one to Betty.

"No," she said slowly, "but don't tell him that."

Carla laughed again. "Okay, I won't. Is there anything you do want me to tell him?"

"Tell him to come move these friggin' crab pots out of the front yard. I want to plant some flowers for a change. But tell him to come sometime when I'm not home. If I see him I still might rip his spleen out and feed it to him raw."

"Okay. I'll do that. Have you talked to the brokerage yet? Do you know what the going price is for halibut IFQs?"

"No." Betty sighed on the other end of the line. "I just don't know why he thinks he can treat me like he does. I'm tired, Carla. I'm tired of working so hard and I'm really tired of not being appreciated for it."

"I know. I'm tired, too."

"I'll bet you are. I saw Jim's new deckhand when I went down to get my things off the boat. She's a doozie. Doozie in a double D cup."

Carla gritted her teeth against the prickling in her eyes. She swallowed and waited as her face grew hard.

"Well," she said finally, "I'll talk to you later. Let me know if there's anything I can do."

"Okay. Thanks for checking on me, but I'm fine. In fact, I feel finer than I have in long while. You take care of yourself, honey."

"Thanks, I plan to." Carla broke the connection and punched another set of numbers immediately.

"Clearwater Brokerage. This is Mike."

She wanted to press her hand over the ear piece. The little bit of Mike that would seep through her fingers would be a great plenty.

"Hello, Mike. This is Carla Marten. How are you?"

"Good! I'm good. How are you? How's Jim? Is he still out fishing? Weather hasn't been that nice. Makes me glad I have an inside job."

"I'm fine, thanks," she answered, leaving the rest to hang. "Say, can you tell me what the market's like for Area 2C Halibut IFQs, A class, unblocked?"

"Oh, real good, real good. Market's real strong, I'd say. Real strong. Are you looking to buy or sell? I'd say it's kind of a seller's market right now."

"If...if I were looking to sell, what could I get for 40,000 pounds more or less?"

"Oh! Golly, well, like I say, it's pretty much a seller's market, generally speaking, that is. You could pretty much name your price, Carla. Yup, there's not a whole lot on the table right now and quite a few people looking."

She gritted her teeth and pressed her fingers to her forehead.

"Mike, how much would you say it was worth?"

"How much? Gosh! Well, I sold some for a fellow two weeks ago. Let me see...not as big a block as yours. Nowhere near as big a block as yours. Would you have to sell it all in one chunk or would it work for you if I lined up several buyers? Would Jim be ok with that? Sometimes it goes a little faster and for a little bit better price if one person doesn't have to come up with the whole chunk of change. That's a hefty chunk of change, too, 40,000 pounds."

Carla stared up at the kitchen light fixture and shook her head slowly. She saw two dead flies in the bowl. Another buzzed and squirmed in its death throes.

"Carla? You there?"

She took a deep breath.

"How much, Mike?" she said on the exhale.

"Oh, you are there. I thought we were cut off for a minute. So, Jim wants to sell his A poundage. Uh, well, I'd advise starting at nineteen dollars a pound. I know it's a little high. This last sold at eighteen and a quarter. You can always come down a little."

"Twenty seven."

"Twenty seven? You want me to list it at twenty seven dollars a pound?"

"That's right."

"That's pretty steep, but I can run it up the flagpole and see if anybody salutes." A burbling, sneezing sort of laughter came over the line and Carla was reminded of the insect beating its life out against the frosted glass above her.

"Twenty seven, Mike. Let me know if you get any takers. Bye."

She hung up the phone and looked at the clock. 4:30. Mike's ad wouldn't hit the local paper for two days, but Mike was a Moose and if he hit the Moose club between now and dinner, it would be everywhere by lights out. Lights.

She pulled a dining room chair over and unscrewed the glass fixture. Two dried up flies and a newly dead wasp. She smiled. What a surprise to see a venomous wasp this time of year.

Halibut stacking up in the landing checker

"Ray!" Darlene waddled slowly out of the kitchen, still drying her hands on a dishtowel.

No answer.

"Ray!"

There was a startled spasm from the recliner and the plastic popped as Ray pulled his flesh free to turn and look at Darlene.

"Yeah, what?"

"Time to get dressed."

"For what?"

"It's my birthday and we're going out dancing."

"The hell you say."

Ray wedged himself up out of the worn crater of his chair. He stood and put a hand on Darlene's shoulder.

"Happy Birthday, hon. I'm sorry I forgot. I'm just not very good with dates. You know that."

"I'm not interested in excuses, Ray. I'm interested in a dance partner. Go get dressed."

Ray's careful little boy smile grew into a teenage sneer. His grip tightened threateningly on Darlene's shoulder.

"Since when do you tell me what to do?"

"Since I started paying all the bills around here," she said without venom or anger, just plain hard truth. She picked his hand off her shoulder and let it drop. She folded her own arms and set her feet in a boxer's stance. "You remember that little misunderstanding you had with the IRS a few years ago?"

"So what?" Ray tossed his head, "So I missed a filing deadline. I said I'm no good with dates."

"Yeah, three years in a row you missed a filing deadline. They don't consider that a personality quirk, Ray." Darlene's face pressed so close to his that he took a step backward. "They call it tax evasion. If you recall, that's why the house is in my name. And the car and the bank accounts and the credit cards. That's why your paycheck is made out to me, and that's why we're going dancing tonight."

"Why?" he roared more in desperation than in anger.

"Because I said so, that's why," she roared over the top of him. His injured pride tumbled like so many pebbles in the undertow.

"She who has the money pays the piper and she who pays the piper calls the tune. Get dressed, Ray. It's my birthday and we're going out."

Like anyplace, Alaska gives as much as it takes. Alaskan women thought the trade in comfort was well worth the unheard of freedom. They either thought that or they moved back to Ballard.

When Gabriella Hansen's husband had slid into a permanent pool of drunkenness, she had taken over running his boat. At first Leroy had come along, his alcoholic haze tucked around him like a seedy woolen blanket. Then one morning he had missed ship's movement entirely. She stormed up and down the deck flinging curses at the deckhand in an indistinguishable but fully understandable blend of Filipino and Leroy's Texarkana drawl. Finally, she threw her hands up in the air.

"Cassoff!" she said.

The deckhand scrambled to untie the lines.

"Summabeech," she growled as she marched into the wheelhouse. She climbed up on the wooden packing case that made her tall enough to see over the iron and oak wheel. She jammed the controls forward and a surprised cloud of black smoke jumped from the stack.

Gabriella captained the *Stormy* for the next twenty years, long after Leroy's liver had checked him into that big detox center in the sky. She pioneered new grounds and modified the deck gear to rely on hydraulics and mechanical advantage rather than brute strength and awkwardness.

Well into her sixties, she would scramble up the iron ladder on the face of the cannery dock like a squat, dark spider. Her vitriolic exchanges with the sorting crew were legend.

"You crazy? Dem's numma one best. Soft? Pah! You go devil, you. Where you suppabisa? I talk him now. I say, NOW! I talk him now or I talka you mamma." And the closeness of the Filipino-

Tlingit community that staffed the cannery made the second threat far more fearsome than the first.

Hers had been an unusual career and unusually successful and she had only tied up the *Stormy* permanently a year ago. Neither age nor infirmity had driven her out, but the terrific push to compete had dulled the joy of it for her.

She had donned her captain's gear before overcrowding and over harvesting had driven fisheries managers to impose strenuous gear and season restrictions, limited entry, and IFQs. The wide open ocean had long since been fenced, gated, and padlocked. Layers of regulations and treaties had grown into a mind boggling maze that challenged the ingenuity of the average fisherman, but that only meant the average fisherman had to fish--and scheme--harder.

Not so many years ago one enterprising fellow asked his girlfriend to hold one of his several permits in her name. When she walked in on him entangled with another woman, she refused to return the permit although she did give him back his black lab which had just shredded the inside of his van and pupped a litter of twelve on his clean laundry. Instead she bought herself her own boat to go with the permit and became a highly independent and successful fisherman. The men in town laughed nervously. The women howled at the justice of it. However entertaining, it was considered an isolated case. Usually when men lost IFQs and limited entry permits it was to the grasping clutches of the IRS or at the order of a divorce court.

What Betty Dahlberg and Carla Marten were doing set a dangerous precedent. No divorce, no court order. They were taking IFQs placed in their trust and treating them as their own and purely for personal spite. No one knew how many families hid their holdings in similar arrangements. Like prostates and sexual preferences a generation ago, such dealings weren't discussed outside, but infant daughters owned gillnet permits, toddlers who couldn't lift a fish owned the rights to catch them, and crab permits were passed around fishing families like measles.

IFQs were relatively new and the full devious power of the fish pirate had yet to be tried. This new twist caused the pirates to stroke their beards thoughtfully.

Mack Harrison stroked his beard as he sprawled liquidly over a kitchen chair. James Taylor crooned in the background as Mack pretended to read the paper. The most important news item, one line in a brokerage ad, had already raced like a gasoline fire down every dock in the harbor. He eyed the ad again.

40,000# A Class Area 2C Halibut - $27.00/lb. OBO.

His eyes shifted to where Kathy, his wife and partner in their gillnet business, played on the floor with their two fawn like daughters. Both girls had Kathy's big brown eyes and wild limbs that would one day be tamed to dance. He squinted and pulled at his beard. Were Kathy's eyes soft and brown or dark and dangerous? Was she a sunny Mediterranean French/Italian or something far more sinister?

He twisted the coarse facial hairs and felt one come free in his hand. He twirled the wiry bristle in the sunlight. She hated this beard, said it poked and scratched rather than tickled and teased, and had often asked him to cut it. But he had grown it during his college days and kept it now out of stubbornness, as a symbol of his independence. In truth, he knew he was just too lazy to keep shaving every day.

Kathy looked up at him as she eased their youngest from one leg of her lap to the other. She tossed him a lazy morning smile and returned to the wooden puzzle on the floor. He watched the sunlight pool around them. He felt their laughter clutch at that soft place behind his sternum.

The radio switched to a Joni Mitchell song. He watched Kathy rock to the jazzy melody. She mouthed the words, sometimes singing softly into her daughter's ear, "Don't it always seem to go/you don't know what you got till it's gone."

Abruptly he stood and left the room. Moments later the grind and snap of scissors could be heard from behind the bathroom door.

Warren Olsen leaned both elbows on the glass counter. He timidly tapped buttons on the machine before him and the chart display zoomed in or out accordingly. He was mesmerized by the possibilities it set swimming in his head.

"So this shows you where your boat is on an electronic chart at any magnification you want?" he asked.

"Right! It interfaces with your GPS and, if you want, your autopilot. You just tell it where you want to go and it takes you there."

"And you can record your sets and drags and pot strings?"

"Absolutely. You can also keep your log book on the word processor."

What they were discussing, huddled like two small boys over roadkill, was a laptop computer with interfacable navigation software, the latest in marine gottahavits.

The salesman looked up as another customer came in toting a radio the size of an old fashioned breadbox under his arm. Sooty fingerprints edged the case like black lace.

"Excuse me," he said and left Warren with the machine.

"This is fantastic!" Warren said to himself, already picturing where in the pilothouse it would live. He was scrolling down a list of charts on the CD ROM when the mournful voice of the radio customer cut through his euphoric haze.

Earl Dahlberg, with red rimmed eyes and hair squirrelled in every direction, moaned like he was gutshot and complained to the clerk that he couldn't afford a new radio. Not now. Especially not now. Not with the mess he was in. Well, then, he certainly couldn't afford to repair this one, the clerk replied. Why, he'd have to send to the Smithsonian for parts.

The clerk laughed at his own cleverness, but Earl and Warren did not. As the clerk reached for a new VHF, Warren looked back at the navigation computer before him. It now looked a strange and insidious thing. His hands pulled away and dropped to his sides. He backed out of the store quickly, watching Earl rock his head back and forth in his hands. He almost ran to his truck.

His eyes only focused clearly again as he was jerking the truck door open. They zeroed in on a poster in a storefront opposite him. A white sand beach, coconut trees, bronzed bodies, and lots of very white teeth. He was drawn across Main Street like a sleep walker. Andy Swenson had to screech to a gut grinding stop to avoid killing him.

"You lucky bastard!" Andy yelled out his window, "I just got these brakes fixed yesterday."

Warren waved vaguely without looking at him and stepped onto the sidewalk in front of the poster. He pictured Marilyn and himself on the beach--a few more clothes, maybe, more modest grins--but happy, especially Marilyn, on the vacation of her dreams. The persistently soggy weather in this corner of America's largest rain forest weighed on Marilyn's normally happy disposition. She didn't complain much, but she did watch a lot of tropically themed house hunter shows on TV.

The cold doorknob in his hand jolted him. He turned to see Earl leave the electronics shop with the new radio, only slightly bigger than a ham sandwich, under his arm. He could see the little blue computer screen staring at him through the shop window. Then there occurred to him an utterly novel idea, bordering, he was pretty sure, on genius.

He would ask Marilyn. Let her choose. And he couldn't lose. Behind Door Number One was the navigation computer and a small stack of brownie points. Behind Door Number Two was a Hawaiian vacation and a veritable Mount Everest of brownie points redeemable at some future date for a navigation computer, albeit some future date when they once again had a small stash of cash without orthodontist or college tuition written all over it.

Warren released the door knob, now warm from his touch, and waved to the receptionist watching him warily from inside. Smiling, he sauntered back toward his truck, but stopped in the middle of the street. He stooped to test a large pool of oil on the asphalt. He rubbed the orange slickness between his fingers and clicked his tongue. Some fool had just popped a brake line and was probably driving around right now without an ounce of fluid in the system. He rubbed the oil absently on his pants leg and walked on to his truck, shaking his head.

"Some people!" he thought as he turned the key in the ignition. "Some people got no sense at all."

EDITORIAL
by Arlen Pinkstad

"We have been hornswoggled, hoodwinked and humbugged." Ah, stirring alliteration there. Arlen patted himself metaphorically on the back. "It is time to salvage what we can from the debacle.

Individual Fisherman Quotas were hailed as the salvation of the fish stocks and the fishermen, but these quota shares have been accumulating in the hands of the already wealthy who drive the prices up beyond the reach of the ordinary fisherman.

What is the next generation of fishermen supposed to do? There aren't many Rockefellers or Carnegies who want to catch halibut for a living, but one needs that kind of wealth to buy enough quota shares to support a business.

It's time to amend the program to make room for people to enter the fishery as others leave. Quota shares should be leased from the government--which is supposed to represent all of us--like stumpage in the national forests. After all, this great natural resource belongs to all the people, and all the people should derive benefit from the harvest. When a fisher..." this was a politically correct but horribly awkward term. He would include it once to show he was familiar with it. "...retires, his quota should revert to the government to be leased by someone else.

It is our opinion that this is a fairer, more farsighted arrangement that will enable the government to ensure that communities like ours continue to receive our traditional share of the catch.

The downturn caused by IFQs is being felt in every sector of our local economy and we must do what we can, sacrifice what we must to salvage our town and our way of life."

A tad too dramatic at the end, thought Pinkstad, and he didn't really address the sticky question of what to do about people like Steve Esterhaus, who had invested everything to buy quota shares, people who had taken that great leap of faith in the capitalist-turned-socialist system. He thought he had all of Neil's main points straight though. But was he too far ahead of the flock? Were he and Neil so far ahead of the troops that they might be mistaken for the enemy? Arlen's back stiffened with resolve. "Someone has to lead," he huffed.

He reread the last paragraph, shook his head and slumped over the desk. Again his fingers tapped the keyboard. He looked up at the clock and let out a hiss. It would have to do. He checked the screen once more, erased a long string of k's at the end, and saved.

Eagle Tree

Standing on her head in the food locker of Steve Esterhaus' boat, the thin voice on the radio came to Holli only in fractured bits. She arranged the cans she thought she would use first on top and listened to her own heartbeat in her ears as the heartbeat of the town filtered down to her. The voice reminded her of the dear distracted librarian from her junior high days.

"There will be a Little League meeting at 6:30 in room 140 of the high school tonight, April 16th. Oh my. Well, I guess that was yesterday. Hope you all made it. Let's see, today: Alaska Trollers Association port meeting tonight at the cannery coffee room. There will be a discussion of the U.S./Canada Treaty and an update on new fishing regulations for this year. All members are urged to attend.

Also tonight, the Writers' Group will host a reading at Marilee Hershaw's home. Readings at 7:00. Refreshments following.

And here's a notice from Syd. It says whoever borrowed the broadswords from the high school prop room for the Viking Pageant last May, please return them immediately. They need them for Macbeth.

And that's it except for the Birthday Book. Today, April 17th, Lyle Corbett and Holli Franklin, neither of whom I know, but I hope you both have a very Happy Birthday anyway. And now...what do I do now, Emily?"

"Weather!" came the faint screech.

"Oh, yes, the marine weather. I don't know who in the world listens to this stuff, but they tell me I have to read it anyway."

After some fumbling, she plugged in a cartridge that in turn plugged the sponsor of the weather spot. "This marine weather forecast is brought to you by Petersburg Chiropractic Center, supporting the backbones of the fishing and logging industries," announced a professionally modulated voice.

Rustling papers reintroduced the elderly volunteer.

Holli sat down on the galley floor with a smile. Her cousin had called her name in to the radio station four years ago when Holli had been visiting for the summer. Each year thereafter, Marie had written her a letter on the day her name was read from the Birthday Book. The letter then always arrived a week after the rush and excitement of her real birthday. It conjured visions of dark spruce hills endlessly marching ridge after ridge into the mist, deep green waters, screaming eagles, seals and ravens and the rich rotting smell of the muskeg. The letters and knowing her name was still echoing around up there kept alive a desire to return to what seemed to her an enchanted place. And now here she was, exactly twenty, with a year and a half of college under her belt and hired on as cook and crew on a salmon troller.

Steve Esterhaus was strapped. Marie had told her so and hustled her down to his boat the instant she got off the plane. He had pushed his hands deep into the pockets of his Levis and looked down at the tarred wooden dock.

"You're green," he had said.

"Green as grass," she had replied brightly.

"But you're sure you don't get seasick." He had squinted sharply at her then.

"No, sir, I never have."

"Green crew doesn't get full share."

"I know that."

He had pulled his hands out of his pockets and crossed his arms, straining his hickory shirt at the seams. He had looked her up and down one more time. She was small, to be sure, but showed more spunk and drive than men twice her size.

"I'll take you on at half share."

"Okay!" She had stuck her hand out and waited while he slowly unfolded. Her hand had simply disappeared into his huge, square paw.

"We'll need galley supplies for eight days. You can charge it to the boat but take it easy. This is a pretty skinny time of year."

"Yes, sir. What shall I get?"

"I said. Eight days worth. I've already got ice and bait. We'll leave on the tide about two. You can stow your gear in the fo'c'sle anytime."

So here she was stowing cans and cartons and cabbages in every nook and niche. For the hundredth time, she pushed her long hair behind her ears and scolded herself for not buying elastic hair bands while she was at the store. Maybe she could borrow a hat from Captain Steve, she thought.

She jumped to her feet as the diesel engine below roared to life. The trap door to the flying bridge opened and Steve looked down, an unbelievably slimy looking baseball cap crammed onto his head. Then again, maybe borrowing a hat from Steve wasn't such a great idea.

"You got everything?"

She looked around and shrugged. "I hope so."

"Okay, cast off."

She jumped over the threshold and ran to the rail.

"Midships last," he shouted down to her.

She veered to the stern, loosened the line from the cleat and threw it onto the dock.

"Hey!"

Eyes wide, she turned to him, wondering what she had done wrong already. He was holding his cap and scratching his blond thatch with one hand while the other rested on his hip. She raised her hands palms up. He leaned against the large iron wheel and crossed both arms in front of his chest.

51

"What were you planning to use to tie up when we get back?" Holli pointed at the loops of line dangling off the edge of the float into the water. She gave him a half smile. "That?"

He returned a half frown with a single nod.

"Yes, that. Go get it. And untie the bowline, too, while you're on the dock."

She slunk over the rail and freed the two lines, throwing them onto the deck of the boat. Climbing back on board, she saw the midships line was looped around the bull rail of the dock and both ends were made fast to the boat's cleat. Now she understood why. She freed one end and pulled the whole line back onto the deck, coiling it neatly and stowing it and the others and in a wooden box Steve had pointed to.

Once free, she stood on deck as they chugged out of the harbor. She tried to look at all the boats, the birds wheeling overhead, the jumble of creosote pilings on which this whole side of town stood, but it was too much to see and smell and feel at once. Too much. She closed her eyes and pulled the muddy, moist, edge of the world air into her lungs.

"Hey!"

Her eyes jerked open and she held her breath. She turned her head halfway around to show she was listening without facing his fury full on.

"Pull up the buoys so we don't look like a bunch of pig farmers and tie them out of the way on the stay poles and how about some lunch?"

She gave him a cheery salute, tied off the buoys, and went into the galley. She laid a scarred and charred cutting board over half of the sink and thereby doubled the available counter space. She was rummaging in the tiny refrigerator for sandwich fixings when they cleared the protecting arms of the harbor. The boat began to buck into a nasty tidal chop and not long after she felt the side to side heave of an opposing ocean swell. The further away from the harbor they got, the harder it became to choreograph the sandwich dance.

Mayonnaise and mustard began to samba on the cutting board then slid off and clanged into the tiny steel sink. They rolled against its sides in rhythm with the swells. She righted them and crammed a loaf of bread into the sink to stop the noise, then turned back around to find the lunch meat.

She felt the boat roll mightily to starboard and splayed herself against the refrigerator shelves. The food held, but on the reverse roll, the door under the oil stove flew open and three cast iron skillets clanged onto the floor.

Closing the refrigerator door firmly, she grasped the lip of the sink to pull herself over to the errant skillets when a violent roll to port pulled her feet out from under her. Scrambling back up, she gaped as a wall of green water rolled toward the starboard windows. She ducked instinctively and was thrown against the refrigerator which, when she and the boat rolled back the other way, emptied its entire contents in her lap.

Apples bounced down the companionway and a stream of milk raced toward the doorsill. Holli struggled to her knees and grabbed the refrigerator door before it hit her in the head. She frantically shoved condiments and cans of soda back onto the shelves, but as fast as she corralled one, another sprang for its freedom.

Then she heard the trap door to the flying bridge open. Steve stuck his head down the square hole. One of his eyebrows rose like a frightened caterpillar and the other slid down in stern disapproval. Holli was slumped against the rocking refrigerator door, ready to bathe in his sympathy.

He shouted over the screaming diesel, "So are you gonna fix some lunch or what?"

Her mouth fell open and her breath came out in disbelieving chuffs. When he had disappeared and dropped the door shut again, she turned and angrily snatched up bruised fruit and gritty vegetables as they rolled within reach. Soon he slid the galley door open and stepped inside. He scooped up what was left on the floor and dumped it in the sink. He reeled off a fathom of paper towels and shoved them with his foot into the corner where most of the milk had pooled. Then he turned to her where she stood braced against the galley table.

"See this?" He picked up the free end of a thick rubber cord that was attached to the wall beside the refrigerator. "It goes here." He hooked it through the handle of the refrigerator door. "This," he shoved the skillets back inside the low drawer and latched a brass hook on the top edge, "this, and this," he did the same on the two other galley cupboards, "all need to be secured before we leave the harbor. Got it?"

"Who's driving?" she asked.

"Got it?" he repeated more loudly.

"I got it. Sorry. Who's driving?"

"Iron mike."

"Who?"

"The iron mike. The autopilot. Ever heard of an autopilot?"

"Yeah, but I didn't realize you'd have one on a boat this small."

He hooked an elbow on top of the refrigerator and glared down at her.

"I mean, this is a nice boat," she said quickly, "I just didn't know you'd have a bunch of fancy stuff."

He nodded his head slowly and silently then, with a flick of his eyebrows and a single dismissive shake of his head, he bent to check their position out both galley windows.

"I'll give you the full tour later," he said, shouldering his way around her, "after lunch."

He climbed up the ladder and onto the flying bridge once again and the trap door slammed shut after him.

"What a grouch!" whispered Holli to herself as she dug to the bottom of the sink to find a badly deformed loaf of bread. She flattened four slices on the cutting board and opened the mayonnaise jar. "Nothing a half a cup of pure cholesterol and a pinch of arsenic won't fix."

Troller at the Foot of the Ramp

Dwayne Dickson pulled hard on his cigarette and made a little popping noise when he released it from his mouth. He dropped it on the asphalt and rubbed it out before turning into the corridor leading to the cannery coffee room. No smoking signs hung on every wall of the room. Defiantly he blew his lungful of poison over the heads of the crowd.

Fifteen years ago, he could have walked across this meeting hall on tobacco smoke. But fifteen years ago, he would have been in the front of the room, not the back, and he would have been the one clearing his throat to speak. Fifteen years ago, he had been an uncrowned prince of the biggest, most successful salmon trolling fleet on the West Coast. Then fifteen years ago, the courts, the politicians, and the tribes had all cleared their collective throat.

Under threat of losing their fishery entirely, Alaska's salmon trollers had agreed to reduced catches in order to rebuild diminished king salmon stocks. It seemed that every year they were expected to bear the brunt of the reductions. It seemed that every year, the regulators expected them to knuckle under, take a pitiful one time check, and quietly disappear. But every year, they continued to gear up and motor to the grounds. It was a way of life as well as a way to make a living and most were loathe to give it up.

He inventoried the membership, a small sea of baseball caps. Some topped gray hair and bifocals, those who had ridden the once lucrative high wave of salmon trolling into the now quiet harbor of semi retirement, and those who had semi retired into it from other more fiercely competitive fisheries. They were men who didn't mind spending hours with their own thoughts, men who didn't mind their own cooking, and men who needed to provide room and a reason for displaced grandchildren and cast off nephews to grow up.

The rest were variously younger men trying to gain a toehold for their families in this entry level fishery. The permits cost a third of any net fishery and all one needed was some wire, a few hooks, and a good bilge pump to keep his rotten zucchini of a boat floating. With a boat like many of these guys had, even the expense of hull maintenance could be spared. Trollers don't need speed and it was barnacles and especially blue mussels that held the whole lot together.

He leaned his own gray head against the wall and looked over at the speaker, a no longer young woman who nodded too hard and laughed too quickly. Twice she had tried to begin the meeting and twice the men had leaned heads closer to continue their own conferences. Dwayne listened in on several from where he stood.

"All my IFQs--and I don't have much, mind you--are in my own name and that's where they're going to stay."

"Damn straight! Even if I can't buy any more poundage, I'm not about to risk what I have by puttin' it in someone else's name."

"Don't s'pose you could make it a legally binding contract or anything. I mean, I s'pose the whole idea of someone else holding your IFQs is kinda contrary to the intent of the law in the first place."

"Too goddam many laws if you ask me."

A crooked index finger jabbed the air just in front of Dwayne. Rudy Valente whipped a woolen workman's cap off his head and slapped it against his thigh. His small, nut brown face was clouded with righteous, socialist anger.

"What everybody seems to forget is, IFQs wasn't thought up to protect the resource. They was thought up to protect the guys as already had from them as wanted in on a good thing. All's it did was build a fence between the haves and the wannahaves, is all IFQs did. Didn't save a single fish, did it? Did it?" he bellowed.

Several heads in the vicinity shook side to side in agreement.

"Doesn't matter if those fish is caught in 24 hours or 24 weeks, does it?" What Rudy lacked in physical stature was made up for in the strength of his convictions.

"All that changes is who's allowed to catch 'em and how far the money is spread. IFQs made sure the money stayed in the hands of them what already had more than they needed. Just made sure the guys on top stayed on top. Just another poke in the eye for the ordinary Joe."

The woman in front finally outshouted them all. One hand on her hip and the other waving insistently, she called, "Alright, alright, let's get started."

Rudy glared and crossed his arms in front of his chest. Decades of brutal work on the fishing grounds had earned Rudy the gentle respect of the fleet. The woman in front could not know that and did not care. Voices dropped one by one until only deaf Tony was left shouting to equally deaf Fred.

"Roosevelt, I tell ya. That's where the trouble started. Perfectly good opportunity to thin the herd, but no! We end up havin' to feed every lazy, no account whiner that doesn't want to get his hands dirty," grumbled Tony.

"Not only we can't afford it, we shouldn't oughta do it," put in Fred.

"I'll take care of my own," said Tony, "see the kids get a decent start, but then, by God, they're on their own."

"That's cold, Tony"

"What? Who you callin' old?"

"Cold!" shouted Fred, "think of all the bureaucrats that'd put out on the street."

"That's exactly what I'm thinking!"

The laughter around them, a slap on the shoulder, a wave toward the front of the room, brought a grunt from each as they, too, settled in to listen--or in their case, watch--the show.

"Okay," nodded the woman, acknowledging their attention, "this is a pretty darn good turnout. Thank you all for coming. We basically have three items on the agenda, then we'll open it up for questions. First, there has been some movement on the US/Canada treaty that I'm going to ask Paul to explain and then there are some new regulations for the hatchery openings you need to be familiar with. Also before you go tonight, it's time for our annual raffle. This organization can't represent you for free and membership isn't exactly breaking any records. Any good records, that is."

She waited for an understanding chuckle that never came. Her eyebrows hunkered down defensively and she continued in a serious, almost menacing tone.

"Everybody should take at least one book of tickets to sell." She waved a fistful of xeroxed tickets over her head. "Hit those guys who aren't members and do nothing but complain about the state of the fishery. You guys have paid your dues and therefore you have the right to complain. Tell them these are bitch tickets--ten minutes a throw. You're going to have to listen to them anyway, they might as well pay for it."

Now the laughter came. Her face lost its glare and her voice lost its edge.

"It's been a tough year--again. I know it's not easy for you guys to watch your livelihood be attacked and slashed at by every government entity around. And I know it's hard to keep supporting this organization when it looks like all we do is defend the rear flanks as we retreat. But you ARE still fishing and you wouldn't be if the tribes or the courts or the Canadians or your own government had had its way.

As I said, there has been some movement on US/Canada. We just got back from another marathon session in Vancouver. I'm going to let Paul brief you on that. Paul?"

Dwayne slipped out the exit, leaving the talk, the tedium, even the raffle tickets behind. He wouldn't be missed. That was the thought that stayed with him as he watched his feet scuff along the concrete hallway. The close stink of the cannery followed him out.

The streets were quiet, newly washed by a passing squall. A few teenage boys joked and jostled each other on the street corners. He passed Ray and Darlene Cartwright strolling uptown hand in hand. He stepped into the street to let them pass and nodded an evening. They smiled gaily in return. He stopped to watch after them and was reminded of sides of beef swaying in a cooling room. He shuddered a little and turned again toward the docks.

He could still catch the evening tide. He would go looking for spring run king salmon. As he walked his stride lengthened. His lungs filled and flushed clean air. He lifted his eyes to the purpling clouds.

Like many others, he had begun longlining halibut and black cod when the screws were tightened on salmon fishermen and, uncle to Carla, he had also known the ins and outs of the IFQ program before it became law. When the potbellied, pasty faced bureaucrats in Juneau had appropriated a resource formerly open to all and passed out quota certificates, Dwayne had gotten his share. They had reminded him of fat fingered, medieval princes tossing coins to the crowd. The grumbling throughout the state sounded like the forerunner of a massive earthquake, but most fishermen had settled into acceptance of the program and the bureaucrats had settled into their newly created fiefdom, secure behind a mountain of regulations like dukes behind castle walls.

The fresh halibut market was strong and there seemed to be no limit to the amount of black cod the Japanese were willing to buy, and at prices an ordinary fisherman could hardly conceive. The worldwide salmon market was awash in farmed fish and hatchery runs. The prices never had been high, but fishermen now got paid for pink salmon about the same amount farmers were paid for straw. Thus, the few weeks of longlining he did, filling the quota allowed to him each year by the feds, now brought in the bulk of his income.

He stood at the head of the dock. The ramp angled steeply down before him. Two hours to dead low water. He took in a deep breath and closed his eyes against the beauty of the sunset. His broad shoulders sagged as his breath left him. The last cigarette coated the back of his mouth like greasy bilge water. He felt every one of his sixty years and felt a tiny stab of fear as his heart stuttered, a little dance it did more and more often now.

His world was changing, and he wasn't sure he was ready to change with it.

Maybe it was time to get out altogether.

Betty Dahlberg was an uncomplicated woman, gullible and incapable of guile, not a weathervane to be trusted, but if Carla thought Jim's IFQs were worth twenty seven dollars a pound, they probably were. And if she thought it was the time to sell them, it probably was.

He'd wait and sail on the morning tide, but he'd call on Carla first and then, he thought, maybe he'd call Mike Clearwater's brokerage.

His stomach began to roil, but whether it was worry or the spices Myra had used at dinner, he couldn't tell. He turned away and the evening sea breeze lifted his collar and pushed him home. When he clicked the door latch, Myra turned like a child caught with her hand in the cookie jar.

"I thought you were leaving," she said accusingly.

Dwayne stopped over the threshold, his hand still on the knob.

"Well, excuse me for spoiling your plans, but I decided to wait until morning. Okay if I sleep in my own house?"

Myra huffed and turned her head away as though injured.

"You just surprised me, that's all."

Dwayne hung his jacket and hat on the hooks by the door. He stepped out of his shoes and walked past Myra toward the bedroom. Two steps past her he froze. He turned his head, shoulders, torso, hips, and then finally, his legs followed the command of his nose.

"You're wearing perfume," he said in disbelief.

Myra stood unmoving, her back to Dwayne. He slow stepped around her until he could see every detail of her face even without reaching for his bifocals.

"It's new. Do you like it? I was just trying it out." Her eyes flicked across Dwayne's face and moved quickly on.

"And you're wearing makeup," he said, the astonishment softening his voice. "Where were you going?"

She clicked her tongue and let go a petulant sigh.

"Oh, Dwayne, don't get mad. I was going up to the Moose Club."

"To the Moose? What for?" The anger was coiled in his throat.

"Let me finish, will you? Bertie and I were just going up there for a few minutes to watch Ray and Darlene dance."

"What?"

"Really! For the last couple of nights, they've been going up to the Moose and dancing till the sweat pours off them, Bertie says. And they're both so impossibly huge, they look like a couple of elephants. She says it's really hilarious. They're a real hoot, she says. I was just going to go up for a few minutes since I really didn't have anything else to do, and since I thought you had left town."

He could hear Myra's shallow breathing and watch the red splotches forming on her neck and on her face. He could take this anywhere he wanted to. He could accuse her of the hundred imagined infidelities from their accumulated years of separations. He could chill the entire house for days or weeks with fuel like this. But forty years was a deep well to poison. And she had been as alone as he, raised their children single handedly for weeks at a time, weathered a thousand household emergencies, while he was out of radio range.

A deep well indeed.

He laid a hand on her shoulder and felt her stiffen.

"Be a shame to waste make up and perfume both," he said, trying to sound like someone out of *the Godfather*. "Let me change my shirt and we'll both go."

The room was crowded for a weeknight. Every table was occupied. Dwayne and Myra sat with Bertie and her sister very near the dance floor. Dwayne noticed most in the crowd were women. The few men were regulars who had clustered together for protection around the bar.

The band was as tuned as it was going to get, banging out a country and western song about cryin', lyin', or dyin', Dwayne couldn't tell which. Elsie and Albert Thorgesen two stepped Norwegian style in one corner, that is mincingly, as though the Lutheran minister were watching. A young--young being a relative term--fisherman was gyrating with a short haired woman, both of them largely unencumbered by any sense of rhythm.

By far the center of attention though were the Cartwrights. Smack in the middle of the dance floor, they jitterbugged like mating hippopotami. Newton's laws of motion caused them to slip hands often, it being simply too difficult to change the direction of so much mass very quickly, but they always found each other again. They were graceful, as elephants and humpback whales almost always are, basically in time and very much in tune with each other. Furthermore, they were smiling, not smirking like every female in the room, but smiling full toothy grins of pleasure.

When the piece ended, a cheer went up as though a good bit of entertainment had climaxed. Dwayne scraped his chair back and stood. His face was clouded with an angry scowl. Myra looked up at him and said a quick goodbye to Bertie. The band started up again, a jazzy Cajun tune and the Cartwrights decided to use it to catch their breath. Dwayne took Myra by the elbow and led her not out the door, but onto the floor. Myra hung back and shook her head, but Dwayne's grip was firm. At the edge of the floor, he swung her around and took her hands. His face was grim and his movements stiff, but his intent was clear. He leaned his head close to hers.

"Just think of us as the warm up act, filling in for the headliners."

Myra looked back to the table where Bertie sat, eyes wide, hand to her mouth. Dwayne began to sway, pushing her out and back. Myra fought him with passivity until he swung her under his raised arm, flung her to the end of his reach, then pulled her close. She couldn't help smiling up at him and saw his face softening, too. After the second turn and a double twirl behind his back, she didn't care who was watching. They danced like bobby soxers on American Bandstand, missing an occasional cue, but remembering much.

Myra felt years slide away and saw in Dwayne the boy she had fallen for nearly forty years ago, the star forward of the basketball team, captain of the cross country team and prom king. His wiry gray hair sparkled like threads of silver in the dance lights. The strength of him, the grace, almost made her cry. And every thoughtful thing he had ever done for her, every unkind word he had never said, years of gracious compromise and sacrifice rose up and tumbled over her like a tropical wave, washing all the rest away.

When the music ended, she buried her face against his chest and breathed deeply of the sweetly familiar smell of his skin and their laundry soap. The band started up a slow piece and he pulled her away just enough to take her hand lightly in his. He two stepped her gently around the floor. When she twirled slowly away, she eyed him up and down, smiled, and felt herself drawn back. As they swayed and dipped, their legs moved without thought, their bodies fitted into each other, and the music threaded them together.

She recalled an almost forgotten girl, too, that girl of infinite possibilities, of so much potential, that girl she still became in deeply private and awkward public moments. And she did not resent the years in between, the roads not taken, the opportunities foregone. His hand stroked her back and she knew she was exactly where she wanted to be. And she marveled that out of all of those possible lives, she had chosen the single one that had brought her such deep happiness.

Just then he pulled her very close and whispered in her ear.

"Got any Tums in your purse?"

"So," said Dwayne to his niece as he carefully centered his coffee cup on its porcelain coaster, "you want to spit in his face like he has in yours?"

"Oh, no," Carla replied. "I want to see him grovel, I want to watch him beg. I want to see his knees bleed. Then I'll spit in his face. You know, Dwayne, there's nothing I get from him I can't get mail order except heartache and I've finally had my fill of that."

"I'm glad to hear it, girl. But where are you going to find someone fool enough to pay twenty seven dollars a pound?"

"Oh, they don't have to pay, they just have to offer. One offer will be enough to nudge the vise. I've already formed this little corporation. I call it Nutcracker Enterprises. I thought maybe you'd like to be chairman of the board."

Dwayne's eyes widened, then narrowed to slits that squeezed almost shut as an avalanche of laughter filled the room. He rolled in his chair and shook, slapped his knees and coughed himself calm again.

"Ah, Carla." He paused as a few stray chuckles worked their way free. "It would be an honor. A pleasure and an honor, indeed." He took a calming sip of coffee. "Does Jim know his poundage is on the block yet?"

Carla shrugged. "I haven't told him, but you know how bad news travels. If he hasn't heard by radio, I'm sure he'll find out as soon as he ties the boat up. And I'm going to be there to watch him squirm."

Dwayne's eyebrows slid upward. "How long are you going to let him squirm?"

Carla shrugged again. "Not long. I think this time I'm going to cut him loose entirely."

The smile left Dwayne's face. Carla rested her head against the chair back. "I'm thinking it may be easier to be lonely all the time than to find myself all of a sudden abandoned. Easier to hurt all the time than to be ambushed when I'm not looking for it." Tears began to gather in the corners of her eyes but she made no move to brush them away. "I don't know how it got to be this way, Dwayne, but if this doesn't make him sit up and take notice, I don't think I have it in me to try anymore."

He reached for her slender fingers and held them gently between his own rough hands.

"That's kinda what I hoped."

"That this farce is over? That I'm finally ready to leave him?"

"No. That you're willing to try something this crazy to get him back."

The volunteer disk jockey had described the tune as a neo TexMex Cajun Tango, almost as if he really knew what any of those things were and as if he really believed what he said. And although Carla knew he was really only a pencil jockey for the Forest Service, she let the ragged salsa beat of his music bounce her shoulders right and left as it slid around the interior of her new Explorer.

She kept time on the steering wheel and left the engine running after she pulled into the harbor parking lot to hear it out to the end. She powered the window down and let some of the spicy music spill out. It mixed with the mumble of engines and the whine of hydraulic winches. She craned her neck out the window to find the boat. It was in its stall. She could see the guys in the bait shed going through the gear, replacing hooks, untangling snarls, getting ready for the next go round.

When the music ended in an abrupt whoop from the band, it took the disc jockey by surprise and there were several seconds of dead air while he found his headphones and cued up another song.

"Ah, let's take a minute and look at the Birthday Book," he ad libbed while a cacophony of rustled papers and elbows against microphones clued the listening audience to the real state of affairs in the studio. Carla switched the engine off and climbed out. She didn't need to be reminded that today was her anniversary.

She carried a manila folder and when she reached the top of the ramp, she laid it on the rough wooden rail and rested her arms on top of it. She swung her head to take in the ring of steel blue mountains and ice that circled the town on two sides. The harbor below her was a jigsaw of boats, masts, booms, winches, rigging and their reflected doubles, all glaringly bright in the spring sun and all of them as familiar to her as the tidal muck sending up its fertile stink.

68

She pushed away from the rail and strode loosely down the steep ramp. She halloed the men working on their boats and the kids fishing for sea run trout, only ears and eyes visible above the stiff foam pads in their lifejackets.

She slowed down to walk beside deaf Tony, then helped him set his groceries on the deck of his boat. She waited as he eased himself down onto the rail and swung his legs over one at a time. He shuffled toward the door of the low house.

"Tony!" shouted Carla, "Have you thought about taking a deckhand with you?"

He turned with a series of tiny steps and eyed her over the rims of his thick glasses. "You angling for a job, young lady?"

She laughed and shook her head. "No, not today. I have some things I have to take care of. But don't you think it would maybe be a good idea? Just to have someone else along? Just to keep you company?"

"Company!" he snorted, "If I could find somebody who wasn't so damned yappy. I want to be barked at all day long, I'll buy me a goddam dog."

Carla smiled and watched him turn away. "Okay," she called after him, "Well, good luck to you."

He steadied himself at the door and rotated the upper half of his body until he had her in view again. There was no hint of humor in his voice as he said, "Good luck yourself."

Her smile gone, too, Carla tucked the folder under her arm and set off down the dock. The crew ducked nervous nods when she stepped on board and buried their eyes in the tubs of gear. Her mouth became an uncurving line as she dipped the handle on the galley door.

Jim had his back to her, jabbing the tail of his hickory shirt into his jeans. The girl--was this one Jennifer?--had hair that hung forward in a straight blond curtain as she tried to fasten her bra behind her back. She looked up with frightened eyes and let her hands fall. Her breasts

69

bounced heavily like water balloons under her tank top. Carla circled silently around and fastened the girl's underwear.

Jennifer murmured, "Thanks," and seeped into a corner, tucking sheaves of hair behind her ears.

"I was just showing Jenn around the galley. Since she's gonna cook." He turned toward the girl. "But you can go out and help the guys finish going through the gear," he said too fast and too loud.

Carla held up her hand.

"There's no need. Jennifer can stay."

Jim and Jennifer looked at each other across the galley. Then Jim said,

"Look, Carla, it's not what you think."

"Don't tell me what I think, okay?"

She folded her arms across the documents she carried as she watched Jim try to find places for his hands.

"You didn't hire Jennifer to work on deck, or in the galley for that matter. You hired her to work in your bunk." She turned from Jim who was sputtering, "Carla," "Now," and "Don't," to Jennifer and said. "Like it or not, that makes you a whore."

Jim gasped. Jennifer tossed her head and made for the galley door. Carla stepped into the only path.

"You're a whore until he marries you. Then you become the stooge."

"I don't have to take this!" screamed Jennifer.

"No," said Carla smoothly, "but you took it when he offered it to you and that's the way it is."

"Carla, you don't have to hurt the girl."

She whirled on him.

"Why not? Is that your job?"

She turned back and arched her eyebrows inquisitively.

"So, Jennifer, what did he tell you? That his wife just doesn't understand him? That seems to be his favorite line."

70

"No." Jennifer's freckled nose tilted up and her shoulders slammed back to impressive effect. "Actually, he didn't mention you at all."

Carla flinched. Her jaw knotted and her eyebrows became a dark, angry hedge. Jim put one hand on the back of his neck and squeezed it as he looked up at the ceiling. He turned sideways toward Carla and spoke in low tones.

"Can't we do this in private?"

She shot him a look like a sharpened meat cleaver and her words flew like a series of circus knives, each one thwacking deep into heartwood.

"No, Jim, we can't. One, it's never been private. I've never had that luxury. And, two, there's nothing more to do. It's already done." She held up the folder.

"What's that?" His face clouded with real concern for the first time.

"A mere courtesy on my part." She tossed the folder onto the galley table. "It's a copy of the sales contract for my 40,000 pounds of Area 2C, halibut. I've listed it with Mike Clearwater. And I've had an offer at twenty seven dollars a pound."

"You what?!?"

She said nothing. He looked from the documents to Carla to the wide eyed blonde and back to his wife.

"Carla, honey." He held his hands out but didn't advance. "We can talk this out."

"Don't fight me on this, Jim. First of all, there's nothing you can do. And last of all, if we go to court, I'll take everything."

She reached for the door and the latch clicked loudly in the silent space.

"Wait," he said. He sidled around until his back was to the girl and laid a hand on Carla's arm.

"Carla," he whispered desperately, "I love you."

71

All the breath in Jennifer's considerable chest released in a hissing shriek. Pushing Jim aside and careless of Carla's hand on the lever, she slammed the door open, charged across the deck, and scrambled off the boat. Carla pulled the door closed again. She watched Jim's eyes follow the bouncing mass of blond hair down the dock and up the ramp. She placed her hand on his chin and pulled his face to hers.

"I love you, too, Jim."

He focused and his whole face surged upward in a smile, the same smile he had flashed so many years ago over a cherry coke.

"I love you, baby," she repeated, "I just can't live with you anymore."

"MACBETH DOES MURDER SLEEP!" screamed the boy.

Syd's head slumped between his arms propped on the row of seats before him. Slowly he raised his head and breathed a discouraged sigh. He pursed his lips tightly inside of his bushy gray beard then called out, "Elliot! Come here a minute."

The youngest of the Bergren boys trotted across the stage. He had his father, Sandy's height and big, square hands. He also had his mother, Belle's gray green eyes and a hint of her other worldly attachment. The clicking from the lace tips of his untied basketball shoes was clear in the tenth row where Syd sat.

Syd held down the auditorium seat next to him and Elliot jackknifed into it.

"Wasn't I loud enough, Mr. Wright?"

Syd stared ahead as he rummaged in the pockets of his woolen vest.

"Didn't I wait long enough?"

Syd picked the lint off of a foil wrapped morsel.

"How do you eat chocolate, Elliot?"

"What? Chocolate?" Elliot glanced at the stage where the other actors were easing forward at the mention of chocolate.

"Do you cram as much in your mouth as you can without ralphing and see how fast you can swallow it?"

"Yeah. Sometimes."

Syd sighed. He offered the chocolate on the flat of his palm and said,

"Put this in your mouth and don't chew."

Elliot unwrapped it and popped it into his mouth. He rolled the ball of foil between his fingers, ready to fling it like a spitwad except that he was sitting next to the high school principal. Syd took the wadded foil from him and slipped it back in his vest pocket.

"Loll it around on your tongue. Let it mix with your saliva and become a rich, sweet river. Caress it. Feel it melt, buttery, intoxicating."

Syd saw the boy's jaw muscles flexing. His voice assumed the snap of a hedge clipper.

"Don't chew, Elliot! Relax. Close your eyes. This isn't a race. The pleasure is in the journey, not the destination. Do you feel the velvety chocolate sliding down your throat?"

The boy nodded.

"Shakespeare is like chocolate, Elliot. Every phrase is a sweet morsel to be savored and enjoyed. It should roll off your tongue like chocolate rolls down your throat. It doesn't do anybody--not you, not your audience, certainly not your director--any good to get to the end of Act IV if you haven't enjoyed the journey through Acts I, II, and III. Do you understand me, Elliot?"

The boy nodded again.

"Okay. Let's try it again from the top of page forty. Page forty, everybody," Syd shouted.

The players shuffled back to their spots. Elliot bounded forward and leapt onto the stage, scooped up his script and took his place.

"Okay," said Syd.

Elliot took a deep breath, leaned his head back, and exhaled.

"Macbeth...does...murder...sleep," he drawled, like Brando in a coma.

Syd sprang to his feet and swung his fist in the air.

"Chocolate, Elliot! Not molasses!"

"Macbethdoesmurdersleep!" Brando on barbiturates.

Syd stood granite faced in row ten. Elliot shifted from one size thirteen to the other, glanced at Syd, at his script and tried again.

"Macbeth does murder sleep?" Brando in psychoanalysis.

"Elliot," shouted Syd, "all of you, take these words and make them your own. Steal them. Shakespeare's been dead for 400 years. He won't mind. Possess it. Screw your courage to the sticking place, grab it by the throat and make it yours!"

Elliot exhaled, inhaled sharply and filled the auditorium with agony.

"Macbeth does murder sleep!"

"Good, Elliot! Good! Go on!"

Not Burton, thought Syd, not even Brannaugh. But Brando bellowing balefully in basketball shoes will do.

IFQs or no IFQs, Earl or no Earl, Betty had never had any intention of moving Neil Esterhaus into the family home. Neil had merely insinuated himself into her dinner routine after Earl left, and because the scandal of their brief high school romance was yesterday's news to most of the town's unofficial historians--she had been nearly three years older than he, after all--even one dinner was far in excess of the requisite needed to fuel the gossip mill.

They sat now at the corner of her family's table, a study in contrasts, he of beauty withered, she of beauty weathered.

"Of all the places I've lived, San Francisco was the best," sighed Neil. He stretched until only his shoulders and buttocks rested on the chair. His legs reached far under the table and crossed at the ankles.

Betty pulled her own legs out of his way, hardly moving the tabletop triangle of elbows and chin.

"And why is that?"

"Seattle is nothing but a giant suburb. Lawns and trees and one boring little house after another. Portland's worse and L.A. is full of cons."

"Cons?" she asked. She shifted her plate to the side and smoothed the tablecloth beneath.

"Con artists," he said. His eyes roamed the city streets he seemed to have found on the ceiling. "You always have to be on your toes and paying attention, just to stay alive. But in Frisco, you are on your toes because you don't want to miss anything. So much is happening all the time. Opportunities. Everywhere. Opportunities."

She stacked her dishes and the serving pieces into an unstable pile as Neil nodded slowly, lost in thought. She watched him without speaking for some time, then scooped up his dishes and added them to the rickety tower.

"Coffee?" she asked.

"Sure."

She carried several loads into the kitchen while the coffee burbled in the machine. Once the table was clear before him, Neil leaned forward on his arms and asked, "Don't you ever want to get off this damned rock?"

She gathered up the wadded paper napkins and stood behind her chair, wrists resting on its back. With sarcasm but no bitterness, she said, "Oh, but we do get off every summer."

"Yeah, I'll bet it's a real picnic, too."

She tilted her head to one side, examined a far corner of the room, then nodded. "Yes, sometimes it is a picnic. Sometimes it's a barbeque. Sometimes it's just a couple of hours beach combing while the fish aren't biting."

She focused once more on Neil, smiled, and walked back into the kitchen. She poured two cups of coffee. As she set them on the table, she said, "But the real question is, why did you ever come back to this damned rock?"

"Well, when I came back for Dad's funeral," he eased the cup to his lips, but found it was too hot, "I took a look around and decided it was time to drag this town into the twenty first century. I had just wrapped up a senatorial campaign and my guy blew it at the very end, so there was no job waiting for me there." He tried the coffee again and managed a small sip. "And Mom is getting older. She needed some advice on managing the assets Dad left behind."

"Opportunities," nodded Betty.

"Opportunities," smiled Neil.

Everyone had heard about the advice he had given his mother from Myra Dickson whose nephew, a probate lawyer, barely saved Berle's estate from vanishing down some mysterious, tax sheltered, sure fire rat hole. "That reminds me," he added, "let me know when you're ready to move on those IFQs. I've got a sweet deal simmering on the

back burner. Double your investment in six months. Guaranteed."
He raised his cup again and, eyeing her over the rim, asked, "You
ready to sell?"

Betty did not look at him. She only reached for the milk pitcher
and said, "Your mother must be very lonely. She and Berle were
good friends."

Neil's arm hesitated a moment in mid air. "I suppose so," he said
vaguely, burying a small nod in his coffee cup. After a delicate slurp
he added, "Speaking of friends, I haven't seen Suzanne Gunderson
since I've been back? Is she still around? Whatever happened to
her?"

"Oh, my! I haven't seen Suzanne in years," answered Betty. She
stirred milk into her coffee and watched the billowing clouds blend
away to sameness. "She married twice, you know. Three times
actually. First Kenny Baldwin, but that didn't last long. She couldn't
handle all the time alone while he was out fishing. Started fooling
around some. They divorced. He was so angry, I don't think he ever
got over it. Never did marry again so far as I know. He went out with
every eligible girl in town—and some who weren't so eligible. He
finally decided to keep a woman in Bellingham. Sort of a high class
whore."

She spoke matter of factly and Neil's eyebrows edged up on his
forehead.

"Suzanne now," Betty sipped her coffee and gazed into the steam
above her cup. "Suzanne married Al Couverden. He used to
mechanic for the logging outfits when there still were some of those
around. You remember him. He was Golden Gloves champ while
you were in school. Built like a fireplug. He wasn't fast or even very
cagey, but no one could budge him. He'd just wear them out until
they couldn't hold up their arms anymore, then he'd land a Sunday
punch and that was that."

"I remember him," said Neil bitterly. "I was scared to death of him. He terrorized all the underclassmen. Stuffed Ole Berhardt's head in a toilet. Tied Erling Mikkelson up, taped his mouth, and lowered him out the window of the Biology room. Left him dangling there the whole period. Mr. Skinner never noticed the rope or that Erling was missing. Yeah, I remember that stupid ape."

"Yes, well, slow and steady and a little bit mean, but at least he was home every night. That's what Suzanne thought she wanted, but after a couple of years, Al was driving her crazy. Absolutely crazy. She was afraid to ask him for a divorce, so she up and ran off with the Baptist minister."

"No kidding! Where is she now?"

"Someplace in Idaho with a whole passel of kids, I heard. But the best part is that Al and the minister's wife ended up getting together and she made a new man out of him." Betty chuckled and set her cup down. "I once saw her back him into a corner at the hardware store, calling him names that'd make a sailor blush. Finally he slunk off to do whatever it was she wanted him to do without a word. Practically saluted, too." She shook her head. "I tried not to watch, but I have to admit, it was a sweet moment."

"I lived in Idaho for a couple of years," said Neil. "What a bunch of yokels! I ran a general mercantile there. We had guys coming in there with belt buckles bigger than their heads, and definitely bigger than their brains. I got out of there as soon as my contract was up."

She smiled down at her coffee cup. "Where to then?"

"Portland. Another yokel town, but a hundred times more savvy than Pocatello. You know, I saw a girl in Portland once that reminded me of you."

"Really?"

"Really! She was getting off this bus. She had a couple of suitcases and she just got off the bus and looked all around like she'd never seen a building more than three stories high. And I thought to myself, 'this kid's gonna get eaten alive.' And no sooner had the bus pulled away than some little gangster ran up and grabbed her purse off the pile of suitcases and disappeared."

Betty drew a slow, deep breath. She pictured the stack of tapestry cases Sheryl had received at graduation and the soft glove leather handbag, her own going away present to her daughter.

"What did you do?" she asked quietly.

"I laughed. It was probably the cheapest in a whole string of lessons that sweet young thing was in for."

Neil laughed again remembering. Betty slowly replaced the salt and pepper on the robin's egg blue ceramic tray Earl Jr. had made in middle school. Its uneven legs thumped against the table as it found its balance point. Then she asked Neil, "More coffee?"

"Better not. Better be on my way actually. Thanks for another wonderful meal."

"You're welcome." Her voice was cool.

"I'm racking up quite a debt here."

"Forget it, Neil. Been nice talking to you."

"Are you sure I can't take you to dinner sometime?"

Betty only smiled. "Where, Neil? Since the cook at the Elks club got picked up for dealing cocaine, there's really no place to go. Thanks for the thought though."

She walked him to the door and waited on the front porch while he carefully negotiated the seldom used stairs. He and Earl were the only people besides a pair of Mormon missionaries to have used them in the last year. Friends came and went by the back door.

The evening was clear with a promise of summer in the light breeze. She crossed her arms and watched the sun stroll down the side of the mountain across the way as it always did for a few days at this time of year, like a hiker heading back to camp.

When Neil had been escorted a hospitable distance toward town by her uncurious eyes, she closed the door behind herself and went to face the sink full of dirty dishes.

There had never been a question in either Earl's or Betty's mind as to whose house this was. Her parents had built it on the point when there was only weather and wildlife around them. Now it was shoehorned in between view hungry latecomers and stood forever in shadow. A road had gobbled half the shore width and cut the house off from the sea. Diminished, hunched, the house brooded darkly through its narrow casements.

Norwegian through and through, Betty's father had done things in the traditional way. He had bought as many doors as he could afford, stood them up on the site, then built the house around them. It created lots of tiny rooms with a few poorly placed windows, but Betty was used to it. Most of the unnecessary doors were off their hinges now and stored under the beds. She had had Earl widen two doorways and knock out a wall and that had helped. Quadrennial layers of wallpaper, each one lighter than the one before, and numerous lights added over the years had brightened the place to tolerable.

In truth, Betty didn't much care anymore. The kids were raised. Earl was gone. All she needed was a quiet place to think. With Neil fed and sent on his way and her dishes done, she walked through the house, slowly turning off lights as she went. She lowered herself into a rocker by the front window, reached up and switched off the lamp beside her. The square of window popped from deep black to early dusk.

She rocked and watched the last flashes of day on the rippled waters, like music, like a bird call, repeating, repeating, every time a little different, and gone forever. It seemed the colors of the sky were

81

not just reflected by the water. They were absorbed, altered, and given back, like memories, real events absorbed in every detail, but returned to consciousness changed. The heat of the day came back diminished, the smell of the grass enhanced, joys equivocated, fears distilled, loves diffused, angers softened. Most particularly, she found that the angers had softened.

A troller's wake fractured the water surface, creating an undulating carpet of diamonds and sapphires. Betty raised the binoculars to her eyes, but it was too dark to make out the name on the bow. She set them down and picked up the bowl of sea shells beside them.

With one finger she stirred the delicate scallops, tiny crabs, clams, mussels, miniature abalone, starfish, and sand dollars collected from a sunny sheltered cove with no human trace but their own. That day, Earl had pulled the gear, anchored, and gone hunting nearby. Betty had taken most of her clothes off and let the sun paint her white body hot pink. The kids had brought her these stranded treasures as the tide sank hour after hour. The sill was full of glass floats, twisted driftwood and trophy shells from other beaches and other afternoons stolen from the daily grind and she remembered every one of them. Of everything though, these miniatures were her favorites.

She picked out twin scallops, each less than half an inch across and laid them side by side on her palm. As delicate as a baby's ears, as pink as spring roses after all this time, she held them to her own ears and turned toward the darkening pane. It mirrored her back, tinged blue with charcoal eyes and deep furrows either side of her mouth. She returned the scallops and picked up a mushroom colored starfish. She laid it on her breast and the dried stubble feet clung to her sweater. Ignoring the creased face above, she admired her brooch in the window. A last flash of sunlight bounced off the water and touched the reflection where the starfish shone for an instant brighter than cut crystal, brighter even than diamonds. She pulled it carefully free, replaced it in the bowl, and replaced the bowl on the sill.

Her eyes were drawn once again beyond the panes to the stained gravel patch where their old Chevy pickup had been hemorrhaging oil and rust for years. Kernels of shattered safety glass outlined where the truck had stood. A series of black splotches marked where it and a sad series of beaters had corroded uncomplaining into oblivion.

Betty laid her head back against the worn wood of the chair and let a long trail of breath escape her. She sat and rocked and saw not the procession of ceiling tiles before her but a procession of seasons; herring season, halibut season, crab season, salmon season, maintenance season, herring, halibut, crab, salmon, maintenance, herring, halibut...

She stopped rocking and said aloud, "Maybe just the Buick."

It was very quiet in the house. The silence massaged her skin like gentle hands. She began to nod slowly.

"Yes," she said, "I think we could just manage the Buick."

She rolled forward and pushed herself up. She made her way through the house without turning on any lights. She knew every obstacle by heart.

Beach combing when the fish aren't biting

As Neil strolled the short way back to town, his attention seemed to be on the click and screech of gravel beneath his glossy shoes. Some things had changed, he thought. The city noise of leather shoes on concrete was new. The sidewalks of his childhood, indeed many of the streets then, had been planks. They were always treacherously slick when it rained as it often did, but at least the gravel fell down between boards that gave you a spring in return for each step instead of this desolate, unyielding crunch.

There were more outlanders now, too. It used to be almost every name ended with a -berg or a -dahl, a -vik, -stad or -sen and a core of a dozen or so families regularly united blonde headed offspring in solemn, predictably identical rites destined to create a new generation of Bergdahlvikstadsens. The bloodlines had thinned and the Pentecostals were on the rise, but there were still enough pure Norwegians left in town to preserve and defend its legacy of fairy tale cleanliness. He liked that.

He glanced up from his feet and into the lighted windows of the house above him. Sandy Bergren, chairman of his store's board, paced and flung his arms wildly in front of an invisible audience. Neil smiled. Yes, some things had changed. And if he continued to gain support like a magnet cast into a drawer of iron scraps, many more things would change, too. It was a small kingdom to be sure, but a crown is a crown and he already felt its chill weight circle his head.

This scheme, this IFQ plan may not be brilliant, may not even fly, but his hope was that it would be enough to propel him into a seat in the state legislature, maybe even the state senate, then, with any luck at all, to Washington D.C. Neil had long ago decided that work was intended for other people and a plush leather seat in the plush carpeted halls of government was just the sort of plush nest he planned to inhabit and the sooner, the better.

He glanced again at the windows above. He knew Sandy didn't like the plan, knew he didn't trust Neil to have anyone's best interest but his own in mind. But he also knew that most people didn't pay enough attention or think things through far enough to see where it would all end up. It sounded good and that was all he needed as a stepping stone out of this backwater and on to better things. He smiled to himself as he crested the small hill and dropped down into town.

Inside the home above, Sandy's audience was not invisible, just small. Belle sat like a fragrant heliotrope, her legs curled beneath her as the sun arced across the living room, spun, shouted, and paced its course again and again.

"It all buzzes around in my head until I don't know which way to turn or what to think. What business does the store have getting into fish politics? I don't even know what business the store is in anymore. Your father would have known what to do. But then your father lived in simpler times."

"My father was a simple man," said Belle. "He fished and made sure the store had what he needed to keep fishing."

"Times have changed, though," argued Sandy. "The town has changed. Or we've changed the town. I don't know which. But I walk into that store and see all the tea towels and crystal and tourist geegaws and I want to scream. Who are we, Belle? Who do we want to be? Are we Neil Esterhaus or are we Stevie Esterhaus? I don't think we can be both."

Belle shook her delicate head. "You're you, Sandy."

He stopped pacing and fell to his knees in front of her.

"That's all I am," he cried. "That's all I am, and if you love me, that's all I need." He buried his head in her lap.

"Of course, I love you," she said as she ran her fingers through his hair. Sprigs of white were beginning to appear in those dark curls, but all Belle saw was the power and the passion rising off him in shimmering waves.

"And I'll never be slick like Neil," he said, looking up at her.

"No, never," she agreed.

"And I don't think this town wants or needs to be just like every other town in America. When you walk into our store you should get some idea, you should know where you are. You should be able to look at our shelves and understand the whole reason this town exists. You should be able to see it and touch it and smell it and get good and greasy from it. And as messy, as cluttered, as unscientific as that may be, it's who we are."

Belle smiled into his eyes, now level with hers.

"I'm going to move the marine hardware back downtown," he said, "back by the docks where it belongs and Esterhaus can put all his computerized, double cross check inventoried, state of the art, prepackaged, we-know-better-than-you-what-you-need crap into the store up on the hill.

When a person needs vacuum cleaner bags or a three ring binder, it doesn't really matter what part of town he comes from or how he gets to the store, but when a fisherman needs a 5/8 inch lag bolt or fifteen fathoms of line, we know he's gonna walk up the dock and cross the street and go straight to our store like he and his father before him and his father before him all did."

Belle nodded her delicate head slowly.

"That store has always been the heartbeat of this town," he went on, his voice gathering steam, "and to replace it with a whole truckload of phony little goddam tourist trinkets is like ripping all our hearts right out. At this point I don't really care if the store makes money or not. It will either way. I just can't see turning my back on everything we are and have ever been. I'm not ready to lay down and lick the boots of every spawned out tourist that staggers into town. What do you think, Belle? Am I wrong? What do you think?"

"I think you knew all along what you wanted to do, but it was sweet of you to talk to me about it."

She pulled her legs free and they both stood.

"Ah, no, Belle. You see everything so clearly. You make everything make sense to me. I think we ought to trade places. You go run the business and I'll stay home."

"Don't be silly, darling," she said. "You don't know the first thing about roses."

He blinked. She brushed his cheek with a tiny kiss as she pulled on her gardening gloves and picked up the shears on the kitchen counter. She walked to the back door and paused. Turning to look over her shoulder, she said simply, "Come on," and he followed, not even asking where.

"You're killing me here, Carla."

"Oh, yeah?" She nodded her head in amiable agreement, "Well, we all gotta go sometime." Then she cocked it sideways, "Only question is, do you want to go fast, or do you want to go slow like me?"

The red ember of her cigarette crackled in the still room and baby doll dimples in her cheeks deepened into ravines as she inhaled. She pulled the cigarette away and, squinting at him as though from a far distance, blew a choking cloud into the air between them.

Jim perched on the edge of the same cushion in the same miserable way Earl had a few days before, his forearms draped over lanky legs. Once again, the odor of diesel and old rubber filled the air. Carla waited, her own legs crossed and wrists dangling over the arms of a brocade lounger. Smoke from the cigarette in her right hand snaked up her arm and broke into a lazy spiral. Jim's lips parted and he drew breath, but no words followed. Instead his eyes slid from one part of the room to another, never finding a fixture or a picture frame or a fabric with enough of him in its texture to hold on to.

"I liked our old house better," he finally said.

"Really?" she replied calmly, "This one's easier to keep clean."

"Carla," he blurted, "What do you want me to do? I said I was sorry. I fired the girl. What the hell am I supposed to do now?"

"I don't care." The three words landed like a neat row of bricks between them.

"What do you mean, you don't care?" His voice rose, red and raw in the silk and ivory room. "You've got me pinned to the wall and you're sticking it to me. What do you want? What do you want me to do now?"

She turned her head away from him. Instead she watched the smoke curl and break and followed it to the ceiling. She shook her head minutely. Knocking the ash from her cigarette, she said, "I thought I wanted revenge. I thought I wanted to make you squirm, but then I realized, I don't even want that anymore."

Her eyes bore in on him now, head arching forward on her long neck. "I can't afford to care and I can't trust you. At all. What about last time? What about next time? Jim, I can't do this anymore. I should never have done it. I should have kicked your sorry ass out of here the first time. The very first time. Remember that? Alice Stimson?"

"Nothing ever happened between me and Alice. I told you that! She told you that!"

"Not every affair lands in bed. It was still a betrayal!" She caught the tears and pulled them back before the lamplight found them.

Their eyes locked, flicking right for left. He exhaled. His head dropped forward and bounced as though exhausted. He sighed and reached for the pack of cigarettes between them but she snatched it away.

"Get your own," she hissed, "I don't owe you jack."

Steve placed the tip of a bloody knife under his chin.

"If you nick this artery right here," he said," they'll pump the blood out while they're dying."

Holli lifted the armored gill flap and saw the shadow of a large vein just below the skin. She made one quick slice and dark blood began to ooze and swell with each pump. A large pool of it collected with the slime under the fish. When it smacked its tail against the deck, gooey strings of crimson splattered everywhere. Holli had long since found some green twine to tie up the thick braid of hair that now hung straight down her back, but every night she still brushed long dried scabs of fish blood out of it.

Steve finished running his gear down, the Scottie taking the weight and transferring it to the end of the pole. He turned off the gurdy and hoisted the fish by its head and tail into the cleaning trough.

"Okay." He took a bracing breath. "One." He opened the gill flap again and sliced out the connecting tissue that held the gills. He threw them without looking into their wake. Gulls paddling hopefully astern squawked into the air at the first sign of a splash, but the gills sank away before they could grab them. They paddled closer to the boat and tilted their heads obliquely away, as though feigning indifference.

"Two." He stuck the tip of the knife into the anus and paused while the fish jerked convulsively at the invasion. Holding the wide base of the tail in one hand, he ran the knife up the belly to within an inch of the gills. It fell open as if unzipped.

"Three." By feel only--his eyes were checking each of the four pole tips in turn for bites--he stuck one finger down the throat through the gill opening and, using it for a guide, cut around the diaphragm.

The whole weird assembly, stomach, heart, liver, intestines, eggs, he plunked into the landing checker.

"Now, don't cut too deep here," he said and barely touched his blade to the membrane in the bottom--or top--of the fish's belly. He switched the knife for the spoon blade on the other end of the handle and scraped out the coagulated triangle of blood and the membrane which had covered it.

"Be real careful doing this." He bent his head sideways to peer deep into the opening. At the very back of the cavity three vertebrae grew over the blood reservoir. He cut them and carefully scraped again. The blade skidded over the bones, clunking like a stick against a cyclone fence.

He rinsed the salmon inside and out and slid it into the forward checker. Thick cords of blood slid out the scuppers to the waiting gulls who hiccupped them down greedily. Then milking the gut sac in the landing checker, he poked around in the salmon's leftover lunch.

"Hmmmmmmmm. Hmm, hmm, hmm. Herring, codfish, one squid. I guess our gear's a pretty close match to that." He scooped it all up and heaved the whole mess over the side. Shrieking and crying, the gulls dove on it immediately. The air bladder kept it afloat for a long time and Holli watched the island of guts and feathers bob further and further behind their stern.

"One," said Steve. Holli whirled around and found a fresh salmon twitching in the trough. Steve held out the knife, handle first. Holli took it and expertly sliced and sawed and scraped exactly as her father had taught her to clean the steelhead they caught on the river every summer. She rinsed it and slipped it into the forward checker with the first, then turned to him, her face an unreadable blank.

"Hmmmmmmmm," he said. So what was in the gut sac?"

Holli looked quickly over her shoulder to where gulls bleated and bullied one another for shreds of the unexamined innards.

She shrugged. "Whatever it was, it looks like it was something good."

Steve shook his head without speaking then turned slowly away to run his bank of gear. Holli turned away, too, and rolled her eyes when her back was to him. Steve gazed at the unclouded horizon and almost smiled.

"Saaaaay." Harold let the one syllable do for three, a roller coaster of a word in the best W.C. Fields tradition.

"Did you read the editorial in this week's paper? Why, I never paid good money for such claptrap in my life."

The rattling of newspaper sounded like a small fire had erupted in the studio.

"At least not since last week, I haven't. Here it is. Can you believe this? I quote: 'Quota shares should be leased from the government...and when a fisher...' Don't you hate that? What's a fisher? I say anyone who has the guts to make a living on the ocean is a fisherman regardless of how he or she is constructed under his or her oilskins. Ah, but who cares what I think, eh? Back to the almighty editorial...'when a fisher retires, his quota should revert to the government to be leased by someone else.'"

"'It is our opinion...' you know, this whole editorial 'we' thing sticks in my craw. Just because Arlen Pinkstad has a fancier typewriter than I do, does that make him plural? Or royal? He's a royal.., oh never mind. 'It is our opinion that this is a fairer, more far sighted arrangement that will enable the government to ensure that communities like ours continue to receive our traditional share of the catch.'"

The paper thumped the microphone as Harold threw it to the floor. "And who," he needled nasally, "is going to be in charge of this tidy little bit of social engineering? The same clever Hanses who brought you IFQs in the first place? They're going to decide if you fit their IFQ profile? Do you live in a small enough town? Are you already too successful? Do you have enough education? Too much? Are you too Republican? Too Democrat? Too Libertarian? Do you support the right causes? Part your hair on the right side? Drink the

94

right kind of beer and use the right kind of deodorant?" The phone shrilled in the next room.

"Ah, good," said Harold, "maybe it's Arlen Pinkstad. Both of him."

"It's Mary Margaret," shouted Emily. "She wants to know if anyone has reported finding a ferret."

"A what?"

"A ferret!"

"Not a ferret faced newspaper editor?"

"No, just a ferret."

"I don't know. Tell her I'll check the notices. And while I do, sports fans, here's a little number by Peggy Lee, 'That's Why the Lady is a Tramp'."

Peggy Lee's smoky ballad did its best to sound sultry coming from a cheap stereo on a shelf in the coffee shop.   Just below the shelf was a yellowed No Smoking sign, so nicotine stained it was difficult to read. The music and the cigarettes formed a drifting, shoulder high layer of haze. Below it, Earl Dahlberg and Jim Marten strained toward each other across the small square of formica table top. When the music died and Harold returned, he was ready with notices.

"Well, I have several very important things to tell you." Sarcasm and indulgence, an odd blend aged over time, made the syrup that flavored his voice now. "First, Mary Margaret has lost her ferret. Please call her at 3675 if you see it slinking along anywhere. Then there's the Art Show coming up at the end of the month. Get your pieces to Myra Dickson as soon as possible. The theme this year is 'People, Places, and Flings.' Say, I like that. That could be interesting."

A door slammed in the studio and Emily's exasperated grumble could be heard in the background.

"Well, excuse me! So I can't read your hen scratching. 'People, Places, and Things,' she says. I liked it better the other way. About time we straightened out some of the questionable paternity in this inbred little backwater.   But, here is definitely THE most exciting announcement of all; the high school drama class will be performing Shakespeare's Macbeth next weekend. It says here, 'This is a great little play mostly about greed and guilt, but with enough murder and mayhem thrown in to please even the most die hard Die Hard fan.' Cute. I'll bet Syd wrote that himself. Anyway, tickets are on sale now and will be available at the door, but it's liable to be SRO, folks, so don't be SOL. Be sure to get yours early.

Now," he continued, "Let's have a look at the Birthday Book for this week. On the 2nd, we have Glenda Goodrich, no, that's Baldwin now, Glenda Baldwin. Isn't that right, Emily?"

"Isn't what right?" shouted Emily, clearly nearing the end of her rope.

"Glenda Baldwin?"

"No, you old coot! They flipped a coin at the wedding. She won and they're both Goodrich. Michael and Glenda Goodrich."

"Who ever heard of such a thing?" he mumbled into his mike. "Hummph. Well, one's as good as the other, I guess. Let's see, and on the 3rd, Rudy Valente. Now I know that's right. If he's still alive, that is. Is Rudy still alive, Emily?"

"Oh, Harold, just read the weather, will you?"

Although no one had been pointedly listening to the weekly lovefest between Harold and Emily, at the mention of marine weather, most became still and cocked an ear toward the radio.

"I can read this whole page to you, folks, but it says the same thing over and over for the next three days: Winds light and variable, seas less than 3 feet. Yes sirree, another string of beautiful days in paradise. And now here's a song going out to my Lady Love."

The quiet broke up rapidly as Nat King Cole began to extol those 'Lazy, Hazy, Crazy Days of Summer'.

Earl shook his head firmly, "No, I'm sure the whole thing was Betty's own idea. Carla, she seemed real surprised when I talked to her about it."

"So what's she want?"

Earl's face went blank.

"Betty!" hissed Jim, "What does Betty want?"

One foggy look replaced the other.

"Damned if I know. I can't talk to her. She's all wrapped up in that slimy little Esterhaus bastard. Something about dreams. 'I had dreams' she says. Well, Christ! Don't we all have dreams? I'd like to have a bigger boat, a new string of crab gear, a...say, have you had any trouble with the zincs eating out on your crab pots? I haven't had those pots more than five years, most of them, and the zincs are completely gone."

"When they're in the water as much as yours are, Earl, you should figure on replacing them every three years or so, and I don't think those are the kind of dreams Betty had in mind. Women want foo foo crap--flowers and little presents and fancy stuff like that. Well, you know, Carla buys herself new furniture seems like every couple of years. A guy can't hardly get it broke in and comfortable before it's gone."

Earl nodded his head. "And something about a car. Who needs a fancy goddam car on this island? You can't haul crab pots in a car. You can't even haul much halibut gear in a car. And she'd scream bloody murder if I hauled fish home in the back seat. You know she would."

"I doubt she's thinking about hauling gear, Earl. The real question is, what are YOU gonna do? What are WE gonna do?"

A slap on Jim's shoulder brought him upright.

"So, I hear you two are selling out of the halibut fishery." Sandy Bergren leaned down confidentially. "What is it you guys know that the rest of us don't?"

"Mostly, we know someone willing to pay twenty seven bucks a pound for our IFQs and if you had any brains, you'd sell yours, too," lied Jim defiantly, though unconvincingly.

Sandy nodded, then settled onto the free chair between them. The waitress brought him a cup of coffee and silently filled the other two from her pot.

They all nodded thanks.

"You may be right, Jim. If the feds go for the amendments Esterhaus is pushing, our IFQs won't be worth a politician's promise." He nodded his head to the rear of the restaurant where Pinkstad lounged with the coffee shop regulars. "And that guy's sorry little rag is giving those proposals a life of their own. Did you see his editorial?"

Jim shook his head and answered absently, "No, I haven't had time to look at the paper. Been kinda busy."

Sandy nodded and sipped his coffee. "So how was the last trip? Find any fish?"

"Everything went fine. Cleaned up that little dab left up in Area 3 so I think we're going to take a little time to go through the net. Thinking about going stainless on all the rings. You know if the store carries eight inchers?"

"If they don't, they will. That's what I wanted to tell you. We're moving the marine hardware section back downtown. All that worthless foo foo crap is going up to the store on the hill."

"Great," nodded Jim, "That'll be great."

Eyebrows raised, Sandy turned toward Earl who only looked in confusion from one man's face to the other.

"I thought you said foo foo crap was important."

Jim and Sandy looked at each other and shrugged. Sandy took another long sip of his coffee and Jim leaned over on one elbow.

"Sandy," he said, looking down at the table top, "I know legally Carla can get anyone to fish those shares for her, and there are

98

probably plenty of guys who'd be willing to do it." Sandy nodded and leaned his way.

"Well," Jim went on quietly, "I just hope you won't."

"Won't fish those shares, you mean?"

"Yeah," Jim's eyes flicked upward then dropped to the table where his fingers traced the pattern in the formica. "I mean, I know it's a paycheck for the boat and crew and all, but if no one agrees to fish them for her, she'll have to work something out with me."

"I think I can promise you that, Jim," nodded Sandy, "I don't have time to fit in an extra halibut trip anyway. I don't think most guys do."

"That's kinda what I'm banking on. Thanks."

Sandy lifted his cup one more time, looked at the rainbowed surface in it and set it down instead. He nodded to both men and rose to go.

"Say, one thing, Sandy," said Earl, "doesn't Belle drive a Buick?"

"Yeah."

"How big is the trunk on that?"

Sandy squinted at Earl and said, "I don't really know."

"I mean, could you fit a tub of halibut gear in it?"

"One or two maybe."

Earl sighed.

Sandy shrugged. "See you guys," he said.

"See ya," smiled Jim.

Hauling Dungeness crab pots

Downtime in the Dungeness fishery

Holli apologized silently to the long dead herring in her gloved hands as she rammed the steel needle up its anus and out its mouth. She fitted the loop of a nylon leader onto the open eye of the needle. A shimmering wad of organs hung on the needle's eye when she pulled it and the leader through. She buried one of the three hooks on the end of the leader into the desiccated flesh of the herring, now called a firecracker, and laid it on its bed of salt with the others.

She laid down her instrument of torture and deceit and watched the rocky point glide by. Although the engine cloaked them in constant thrumming noise, she could hear the colony of murres on the cliffs towering above. The rock face was a gigantic patchwork of grays and browns, streaked with white droppings and punctuated by tiny black burrows. The murres perched on shallow ledges and looked like miniature penguins or dove into the water and paddled around like ducks in formal wear. Occasionally they swam close enough to the boat that she could see them underwater, looking then like very sleek torpedoes.

She rested her arms on the rim of the cockpit and traced the horizon. Whales spouted far to the south and a cruise ship, looking from this distance like a top heavy bathtub toy, steamed north. The sun glinted off the glassy water like platters of fire.

One of the pole tip bells tinkled frantically. She spun around and saw the pole itself bow toward the water. At that moment Steve, who was icing fish in the hold stuck his head out of the hatch.

"Jesus H. Christ! Turn out! Turn out! Speed up!"

Holli dove for the controls, pushed the throttle forward and spun the wheel hard to port. Both starboard bells rang frantically now, the poles jerking then bending until they nearly touched the wave tops, actually pulling the boat to starboard against the thrust of the roaring diesel engine. Wires and wood groaned under the load then twanged free. The boat rocked back as though surprised and settled again onto an even keel.

The line from the forward pole tip skipped lazily along the surface of the water. The wire on the main pole that should be carrying the full weight of eight spreads of gear and a fifty pound lead cannonball trailed back, looking suspiciously unburdened as well.

"Slow down!" he yelled.

Holli eased the throttle back down. Steve drug the hatch cover back into place and slammed it down. Muttering and grumbling, he jumped into the cockpit and shouldered Holli away from the controls. She walked over to her side of the pit and crossed her arms in front of her chest. He jammed the gurdy into gear and began spooling wire back on to see how much tackle had been gobbled by the unforgiving rocks below.

He braced his arms on the rim of the cockpit and glared at Holli over his shoulder, then turned away to coil his leaders on the stern. He brought the last of the line up and held the frayed end in his hand.

"Gimme the crimpers," he growled.

She shoved him a pair of pliers already well within his reach and refolded her arms.

"Find me a new swivel."

She opened the parts box and fished out a brass swivel. He took it as he shot her another disgusted glance. Her eyes narrowed.

"Dig out a new cannonball."

"Where are they?" she asked evenly.

"You're fucking standing on them!"

"That's it!" she shouted back.

"That's what?" he bellowed at her.

Holli turned forward and slammed her own bank of gurdies into gear. She began coiling leaders as fast as they broke the surface. He stood with his frayed wire in one hand and the swivel in the other.

"What the hell do you think you're doing?"

"I'm pulling the gear. We're going to town."

"The hell we are!" He reached over and jerked her lever out of gear. "I'm the captain here!"

"You're the asshole, you mean. You don't pay me anywhere near enough to put up with this kind of shit."

"What kind of shit? You ran the goddam boat up on the rocks. You--"

"That tone of voice," she shouted back.

"Tone of voice, hell! You have any idea what you cost me? You ran the boat up--"

"Get off it! You know I don't know the bottom here, had no idea there was a pinnacle out here, wasn't warned," she said pointedly, "and besides it's not the first cannonball you've lost. I'm talking about that sarcastic snarl that tries to say 'You're a fucking idiot.' Well, I'm not. I just can't read your fucking mind!"

She stood nose to chin with him now.

"I agreed to work hard and follow orders and learn as fast as I could. And I've done that, haven't I?"

He stood stone faced and silent.

"I didn't sign on for abuse or to be a toxic dumping ground for your bad moods. Not part of the deal, Bud. Take me to town."

She pushed her lever back in gear. He dropped the wire and pulled the lever back out.

"We're not going to town. The trip's not even half over yet."

She looked at him without anger or malice and without a trace of defeat.

"Fine," she said.

She hopped out of the cockpit and returned his glare with a waxen smile as she unbuckled her oilskins. She pushed them into a bunch around her ankles then bent to pull each leg from around her rubber boots. She gave him one more uncowed glance.

"I've always wanted to take an ocean cruise."

She hung the rain gear on a hook outside the cabin door and disappeared inside.

He leaned against the rear of the cockpit and twirled the swivel back and forth between his fingers. Slowly he ran her half of the gear back down. He looked again at the cabin door then returned to the repair of the other side.

"Hmmmmmmm," he said, "Hmm, hmm, hmm."

He tried not to see her sprawled over the captain's chair on the flying bridge, legs bared to the afternoon sun. He tried not to watch as she brushed back long strands of hair the ocean breeze blew across her face. She had read steadily until the sun had lost its warmth, then she had disappeared down the ladder into the house.

He ran the gear, cleaned and iced fish, pointing the bow directly out to sea when he had to duck into the hold, and set the anchor by himself. At day's end, when he slid the door open and he ducked into the pilot house, the first surprise was that no smell of dinner greeted him. The second was that Holli, now dressed in sweats and an oversized jersey, didn't even look up from her book. She was curled on one of the benches at the galley table.

Steve stepped to the sink and saw the bloody lump of venison steak thawing in a bowl there. He lifted it onto the counter and began washing his hands. He sneaked a peek at Holli's reflection in the darkening glass before him. She read. He raised his hands and turned to dry them on the towel tucked through the refrigerator's handle.

"I guess I'm sorry I blew up," he said.

"I guess you are." She turned a page without looking up.

His square jaw became noticeably squarer.

"Are you working for me or not?"

"That's up to you, Steve. Like you always tell me, there's dozens of guys waiting for a chance on a boat like yours."

"So," he growled, "I just get you broke in and now you want to quit."

Holly reached over her head and tore a corner from the roll of paper towels there. She closed her book on it and laid it carefully on the table. She laced her fingers on top and leaned across toward him.

"I need a job," she said simply, "You need a crew. I'd like to finish the season on this boat, but not if I have to take the blame for everything that happens on it. I figure I make plenty of my own mistakes. I don't need to get yelled at, and certainly not cussed at, for your mistakes, too."

"My mistakes? It was my fault we ran up on that reef and lost all that gear?"

Holli waited for the droplets of the venom to settle to the floor.

"No. You're right. It wasn't your fault. It was nobody's fault."

Holli stared and Steve glared across the small space between them. Finally, she slid from behind the table and, tucking her book beneath her arm, sidled past him toward the fo'c'sle.

"Think about it and let me know in the morning," she said over her shoulder.

"What about dinner?" he yelled after her.

"Thanks. I already ate."

Middle school girls in hopeful dresses guided the town into the auditorium as proper as red nuns. Some perched on wooden chairs behind a library table and a metal cash box, anxiously making change, cocking their heads each time to recheck the hand lettered sign; Adults $6.00, Children and Seniors $3.00.

Some stood by the entrance flashing blue xeroxed papers at every father, mother, brother, sister, uncle, aunt, grandma, grandpa, cousin, neighbor and/or friend thereof, intent that none should pass without a program. Others fussed with trays of cookies and mixed gallons of sticky red punch for intermission.

Freshman boys prowled the light booth. Make up artists, highly trained by Seventeen and Mademoiselle, painted faces with a lavish hand. The high school secretary, her mouth bristling with bobby pins, passed review on each actor. Armed with her office stapler and a roll of Scotch tape, she effected last minute repairs and alterations.

Syd roamed the green room--actually the choir room, just back of the stage--silently bucking the kids up with his exuberantly bushy eyebrows. He glared with mock ferocity, hoisted them in horror at the witches, let them melt at the make up bench and bunched them in stern approval at the splendor of the doomed king. He knew their heads were already too full of words.

In front of the curtain other dramas unfolded. Betty Dahlberg came in alone. Earl watched her, moving only his eyes, as she walked down the aisle and took a seat in an empty row. He mumbled both sides of some argument to himself, glancing at her and wondering why she seemed so different from a distance, since she hadn't been working side by side with him every day.

He glowered and shifted in his seat until he saw Neil enter the auditorium. He immediately jumped to his feet but couldn't squeeze past Ray and Darlene Cartwright who occupied the rest of his row like an avalanche of human flesh. He saw Neil take the seat beside Betty and immediately tilt his head to talk privately in her ear. Earl clenched his fists. He leaned forward to step over the entire row of seats but saw Miss Erskine glaring at him, wearing that same cardigan and those same horn rimmed glasses with the same eyebrow cocked menacingly above them. She held her bony arms crossed before her chest just as she had when patrolling the high school library thirty years ago. Earl slid guiltily back into his seat. He fumed at the blank velvet curtain.

Warren and Marilyn Olsen led their brood into a vacant row, rearranging themselves twice, child, parent, child, before everyone was satisfied and finally settled in. Warren figured he might be adding to his modest and recently depleted brownie point account by coming along when they didn't even have a child in the play. Looking around though, he decided probably not.

As usual, the whole town was here. People who wouldn't walk across the street to shake the bard's hand--himself included--were here. In front of the first row was a short line up of wheel chairs, full of folks who hadn't a prayer of understanding, most not even hearing, this adolescent version of Macbeth. But they were here. Young mothers with children who would have to excuse me, excuse me, their way to the restrooms before the first act was done--they were here. And he was here, too, just because.

In front of the Olsens, Mack Harrison sat with the youngest of his two daughters on his lap. She leaned against his chest and, with a tiny hand, absently stroked his smooth cheek. He rubbed his chin against her fine brown hair and thought his heart was going to burst.

Warren leaned forward. "Say, Mack..."

Mack leaned back without disturbing his daughter or really getting Warren in his line of vision.

"You should drop over to the boat and take a look at the Nav Trak. It's incredible."

"Yeah?" Mack resettled his daughter and eyed Warren straight on. "I somehow don't think it's in the cards for me. I don't do enough trolling to justify it and with gillnetting you aren't always setting on the same spot." "Yeah, but you can play the lines a little closer," said Warren slyly. "You can tell exactly how close to illegal you are."

Mack smiled. "That kinda takes a guy's excuses away, doesn't it? Hard to plead ignorance then."

"True," nodded Warren, "true. But it's great for just navigating to and from the grounds. You know where you are every second and you feel better about turning the wheel over to someone else so you can get a little shut eye."

"That's pretty expensive shut eye. We'll see how the salmon price shakes out this season." He glanced quickly at Kathy, deeply engaged in an impromptu parent/teacher conference. "Wouldn't hurt to take a look though," he said quietly. "You still going be in town tomorrow?"

"I'm leaving on the afternoon tide. Come on down if you get a chance."

Mack nodded and Warren leaned back in his seat, chest high, smile carefully checked this side of a smirk.

In the last row, Marie and her cousin Holli leaned close.

"He didn't actually apologize, but he's been a whole lot nicer since I took the afternoon off."

"He's such a hunk."

Holli shrugged. "It's different when you're working together every day. Tempers get short. You both smell, and you're so tired. It's not like you have romantic dinners by candlelight. You fry something up, choke it down, and fall into your bunk at night."

Holli shrugged again and was grateful for the dimmed house lights. She hoped Marie couldn't see the rising flush in her cheeks.

"I'm just so glad for a day off so I can get away from that boat for a minute. I mean I love being out there. It's beautiful. But it's work, Marie."

"He's such a hunk."

Holli laughed in exasperation. "Okay, Marie, he's a hunk."

"Has he ever, you know, sort of, come on to you?"

"Marie! No! Of course not. He knows better."

Arlen Pinkstad shifted in his seat in the front row. A camera dangled from his thin neck. He jiggled one foot then the other, checked the power level on the camera's battery, and wondered just how much of the play he would have to sit through to get good pictures of all of the major players. An event like this plumped out his paper impressively and upped circulation in order to fill scrapbooks and letters to distant relatives.

The Bergrens, roughly in the middle of the room, held hands while Sandy talked fish prices with the cannery manager in the row behind him and Belle bemoaned aphids to the postmistress in front.

Carla giggled with her aunt Myra, who gyrated in her seat as she relived the evening on the dance floor. Carla shook her head and laughed up at the ceiling. Myra put a hand on Carla's.

"You know," she said, "it may sound silly, but I haven't felt so close to Dwayne in years."

Carla nodded and wiped small tears from the outer corners of her eyes. Myra looked hard at someplace far away. She swayed a little.

"It's almost like you get back into the same rhythm. I mean, you have to, right?"

Carla was still smiling but the smile was tweaked down at the edges now.

"It's like you're back in synch. That's what it is. You're not grinding each other's gears all the time, because you're moving together, making your own music together. I mean, we're still pretty...affectionate and all, but, you know, I think, really, they should give couples dance lessons instead of marriage counseling. I really believe it."

Focusing again on Carla's face, she saw that the smile was gone and her lips were pressed into a tight bloodless line.

"Oh, I'm sorry, sweetie. That was silly, really silly. Silly me. I am sorry."

Myra burrowed back into her seat and opened her program. She continued to shake her head and catch side long glances of her niece. The lights dimmed and Carla could breathe again.

Syd walked back into the green room after taking a peek through the curtain. He said, "Looks like we have a full house."

A murmuration of butterflies filled the room.

"Remember, every one of them is on your side and rooting for you."

He let that sink in. He watched their eyes steady and their chests fill.

"Okay, witches, let's go!"

Each tick of the meter seemed to deepen the furrows on Steve's brow. Diesel prices were up and fish prices were down. The two ate at him constantly. He watched the gallons of diesel mount up on the ancient meter on the fuel dock as he listened to it flow into his boat. He heard the fuel rise into the stem of the tank he was filling and shut off the nozzle. He peered down the filler pipe with a flashlight, then screwed the cap back on. He stood and began to walk the hose around to fill the tank on the far side of the house. Holli stepped out of the pilothouse and saw the heavy hose in a tight bend around the trolling pole. She also saw that Steve was jerking hard to get more slack in the hose.

"I'll get it!" she shouted as she jumped onto the dock. She grabbed the reel holding the hose and gave it spin. At the same time, Steve gave a mighty tug and, finding no resistance, pulled himself and several yards of hose right over the side into the water.

Holli's hands shot to her mouth when she heard him shout and saw the splash. Her neck hunched into her shoulders and she froze for an instant. Then wide eyed, she sprang onto the boat and ran to the far side. Steve's head was just breaking the surface. He gasped and spat and grabbed for the rail, but it was too far above the water.

"I'm so sorry," pleaded Holli as she reached a hand down to him. He took her hand but she could not pull him high enough to make a difference. "I'm sorry. I'm sorry," she repeated.

The attendant strolled out of the shack and onto their boat. He peered over the rail at Steve bobbing in the bay, hair dripping in his eyes and teeth clenched against the cold.

"Kinda early for a swim, ain't it, Stevie?" grinned the attendant.

"Think you could quit laughing long enough to give a hand, Ralph?" he growled.

Ralph and Holli both leaned over the rail, but Ralph was laughing too hard to be much help and, against her will, Holli felt a smile creep onto her own face. "I'm really sorry," she protested.

He dropped both of their hands and fell back into the oily water. When he came back up a salad of seaweed rested on his head. Holli's hands went to her mouth again, but snorts of laughter squeaked around her fingers.

He glared at her and shook his head, causing the seaweed to slip around his neck. Ralph whooped loudly and Holli sputtered, trying to keep her giggles in.

"I'm really sorry," she choked out, "Really I am."

Steve turned away and dog paddled around the stern of the boat to the edge of the fuel dock and heaved himself onto the weathered timbers. He stood with as much dignity as he could muster, stepped dripping onto the boat, and walked silently into the pilot house. Holli bit her lips and watched Ralph saunter back into the shack. She poked her head into the house. Steve had his shirt off and was toweling himself dry. She swallowed at the sight of his bare back and shoulders. She could see his pants were coming off next. She spoke quickly.

"I'm really sorry, Steve."

He whirled. She began to back out. He took a deep breath. "Did you do that on purpose?" he asked.

"No! Of course not. I was trying to help."

"Then it was an accident."

"Yes," she said slowly, "but I'm still sorry."

"It's okay," he said with nearly genuine calm. "It's not your fault." He turned away again.

"And I'm really sorry about laughing."

His head twisted over one shoulder and she saw the ghost of a smile on his face. "That IS your fault," he said.

"I know it," and closing the door behind her, she slid down onto the deck and laughed until her stomach hurt.

Survival Suit Drill

"You're not fixin' to leave on a Friday, are ya, Stevie?"

Steve lifted and steadied a box of groceries on the rail, waiting for Holli to come back out of the pilothouse and fetch them.

"I think I've already had my quota of bad luck for one day, Rudy."

"Yeah, I heard you took a little paddle around the bay this morning," chuckled the old man, "but you'll jinx your whole trip if you leave on a Friday. Everybody knows that."

"I don't have time to worry about it, Rudy. I gotta go today. Season's so dang short any more, a guy's gotta be out there and in the right spot every single minute. I'm not going to catch any fish tied to the dock staring at the calendar."

"I ever tell you what happened to Baldy Olsen when he started a trip on a Friday?"

"That was a Friday the 13th. Today's the 3rd."

Holli took the box and smiled at Rudy. He shifted his weight from one uncertain knee to the other and found his balance again, squinting up at her.

"I'm going up to Fish and Game to get the announcement and then pick up those fuel filters," said Steve. "Stow the grub and don't leave the boat. We're taking off as soon as I get back. And don't let this old buzzard fill you full of dago BS. See ya, Rudy."

Rudy steadied himself with a hand on the gunwale as the finger float rocked beneath Steve's retreating steps. Holli looked down at the gnarled set of sausages hooked over the rail. Each looked as though it had been broken more than once and each had its own story of the old days when everything had been done by hand, nets hauled, anchors lifted, boats propelled, gear built, and fish moved. And all of those tons of fish, those miles of line, those acres of net had left their marks and imparted through the struggle some fragment of their own strength. Knuckles grown large, skin spotted and striped with bluish canals, they nestled together like shipmates used to each others' knobs and quirks and together they stuck out from the sawed off sleeves of his woolen halibut jacket.

"Come on in," said Holli, "and you can tell me about this Friday thing while I put the groceries away."

She went inside and gave Rudy the dignity of her back while he eased crabwise over the rail. He slid into the galley bench in front of the coffee she had poured him. She set the box of sugar cubes beside him and watched while he dunked one in the coffee and sucked the syrup out.

"Baldy Olsen," she said, dropping to her knees and giving the refrigerator a quick evaluation before diving into the maze. "Is that Billy's son or nephew or something?"

"No, no. That's Billy's brother. The Olsen boys, Billy and Baldy are so far apart because Billy's mother died and it took a while before their dad remarried. Married a mail order bride outta Sweden. Real pretty girl, but a mite high strung. Birthed Baldy then hightailed it back home."

"How sad," said Holli, peeking around the corner of the refrigerator door.

"Ah, no. You see, they never divorced really, so Baldy's dad felt he could never marry again. He was a helluva handsome man though and a good fisherman to boot, so there was always plenty of women wanting to keep house for him. Baldy had lots of mothers. Kinda raised up by half the town. Good deal for Baldy's dad, too, if you know what I mean."

One of Rudy's dark eyes disappeared in a sea of wrinkles as he winked roguishly at her.

"I see," she said, smiling into the vegetable bin. "So, I'm thinking maybe Baldy once started a trip on a Friday?"

117

"Oh, yeah. Well." Rudy took a sip of his coffee and grunted. "Baldy was fishing the Fairweather Grounds."

"Trolling?" she asked.

"Yup."

"By himself?"

"Yup. Most of us did then. Weren't no such thing as a season then. Fish were here, you fished. Fish were gone, you worked on your boat. Pretty goldarn simple back then. Pretty goldarn simple."

"So, Baldy..." prompted Holli.

"So, Baldy," continued Rudy, "really hit the fish that trip. Had the boat dang near plugged. Was going to fish just a couple more hours till the tide change and head to town. Then he saw smoke coming out the pilothouse door. Ain't nothing quite so scary as a fire aboard a boat, ma'am."

Holli nodded. Where you going to run to, she thought as she consolidated eggs into a single carton.

"So he runs into the house and the smoke is pouring up from the engine room. He runs down the ladder into the fo'c'sle and slips on the steel steps, smacks his head on the ladder and scalps hisself. Slicker'n a whistle." Rudy ran a hand up his forehead and slammed it down on the table. "Took the whole front part of his hair off. Knocked him out cold, too. When he come to, smoke's still pouring up around the engine room door, so he reaches for the handle and it's so blamed hot he burns both his hands bad. Well, that sobers him up goodly bit. So he grabs one of his shirts and ties it around his head to slow the bleeding and so's he can see. That flap of forehead keeps fallin' into his eyes, you know. And he wraps another one around his best hand and he yanks the door open."

Holli sat back on her heels, lettuce in one hand and a jar of pickles in the other. Rudy slurped his coffee slowly. He dipped another sugar cube and eyed the cookies on the far side of the table.

"Help yourself," said Holli quickly, "Please." She waited impatiently while he dunked and dunked and dunked his cookie. At last, he looked over at Holli. She raised the lettuce encouragingly.

"Well, the whole thing was burning like Hades itself. He got a fire extinguisher and put the worst of it out and smothered the rest with his bedding. Thing is, all the wiring was burned up so he couldn't start the engine and he couldn't call for help. So there he was."

Rudy sucked the coffee out of his cookie and shoved the mushy remains in his mouth.

"How long was he out there?"

He nodded slowly as he chewed, took a long pull from his cup and said, "Oh, he drifted around for a little over a week, I guess. His head festered all up and never did heal up right. He looks kinda like that Klingon fella on Star Trek whenever he takes his hat off which I can tell you doesn't happen very often. That's why they call him Baldy. His hands swoll all up like a pair of boxing gloves. And on top of that, by the time he was towed to town, his fish was all sour and his wife had run off with the traveling dentist."

"Oh, no! How terrible!"

"That's why don't nobody leave here on a Friday. Course, used to be, wouldn't nobody take a woman on board neither. Real bad luck. Nothing personal, ma'am."

"No offense taken," she said with a smile. "Anything else I should know about? Any other superstitions?"

"I wouldn't say they're exactly superstitions. I mean, it only makes sense not to have dirt on board. Boat's going to naturally want to go aground then. And whistling. Don't never whistle. You'll whistle up a storm. Or cook split pea soup. We call that Southeast Soup. Bring on a storm sure as anything."

Holli quickly shoved two cans of pea soup into a locker where Rudy couldn't see them.

"And you don't never talk about longfaces."

"Longfaces?" asked Holli.

Rudy looked around as though spies had sneaked into the small cabin without their noticing. He bent toward Holli and whispered, "Horses."

"Horses!" she snorted.

Rudy tried to shush her and searched the corners of the cabin again nervously.

"Why ever not?" she whispered.

"I don't know, ma'am. I just know it's real bad." He began to inch toward the free end of the bench. "And no umbrellas and definitely no suitcases," he said nervously. He slid off the bench and made his crooked way over the threshold. He turned when he reached the rail. "And of course you wouldn't ever say the ugly number."

Holli stood in the doorway with her arms crossed. "Of course not," she nodded. Then leaning forward confidentially, she whispered, "What number would that be?"

"A baker's dozen, you might say."

"Ah hah! I'll remember that."

"You have a good trip, ma'am."

"Thanks, Rudy. And happy birthday."

His worried face broke into a gap toothed smile. "Thank you, ma'am. And thanks for the coffee. And..." He grabbed the mast stay to balance himself as he eased over onto the dock. "...don't you pay no mind to an old fool like me. That's all just a bunch of old sailor talk. You have a good trip, ma'am."

As soon as Rudy had disappeared down the float, Steve jumped aboard.

"They didn't get those filters in, but we should be fine for one more trip. Let's shove off. You can stow the rest of this stuff once we're underway."

Holli took one more look at the split pea soup as she fitted the lid on the locker, stood and brushed her knees off, then went to untie the lines.

Unloading Troll Caught King salmon

Supervising the Unloading of Troll Caught King Salmon

Carla dropped her duffel bag over the rail then scissored both legs over. Jim ducked through the low doorway of the pilot house and onto the deck. He was wiping his hands on a paper towel.

"You can stow your gear in the fo'c'sle," he said.

She nodded curtly. The freeze out had worked and Jim's was the only boat that would fish her poundage and even then he insisted that she be on board and work a full man's share to get a decent percentage for the IFQs. If he thought she couldn't do it, she was prepared to show him she could and if she thought he would cut her any slack, well, he probably would.

Carrying her bag before her, she navigated the narrow aisle to the steep stairs. She threw the bag down into the dark hole then turned to back down the steel ladder.

The foc's'le was a jumble of sweatshirts, sweat pants, sweat socks and just plain sweat. She found the bunk with no sleeping bag on it, just discarded hunting magazines and greasy, dog eared paperbacks, and cleared it with a sweep of her arm. She laid out her own sleeping bag and put her bag of clothes on top of that.

The boat was already backing out of the stall when she climbed back out of the foc's'le, dragging her rain gear behind her. She snapped herself into the rubberized nylon suit and took one last look at her fire engine red nails. She sighed, pulled on bright blue rubber gloves and took up her station in the aft bait shed, threading hooks the size of a child's fist with body parts of semi frozen squid.

Her hands were small but nimble and she kept pace with the crew tub for tub, each tub holding a skate of 100 fathoms of line with 100 hooks arranged around the rim. By unspoken agreement, the other two left her the spaces on the lower shelves to slide her finished tubs into.

Breaking only for hurried sandwiches and coffee, they worked for most of the twelve hour run to the grounds. In two hour shifts, they relieved the skipper and had all the gear baited before dark.

The sun began to slide behind torn sheets of cloud over to the west, glowing golden then darker and darker orange. As it neared the horizon, the clouds purpled and died becoming ghostly smudges against the deepening sky. Carla leaned her thighs against the rail and, arms crossed at her chest, felt the wind go from cool to cold as the sun finally sank ahead of them. Three ducks flew overhead toward shore and, as magnets, drew another raft of ducks into the air behind them. Even over the engine, she could hear their flat, nasal calls.

She drew a deep, cleansing breath and watched the vague mist of it blend into the dusk. How long since she had been out? How many sunsets, how many storms, how many birds and whales had passed unnoticed? She had felt the unabashed beauty of this place settle into her bones as a girl. It had made her strong, like calcium and magnesium and phosphorus. She was a mirror and a manifestation of the land itself, tall and straight. They were kin, and yet she had let it slide past her for years.

The deck lights snapped on all around her and dusk instantly became deep night.

Jim's voice came over the deck speaker.

"Okay, Barry, we're going to need 300 fathoms on each end. Let me know when you're ready."

Barry and Josh dropped their cribbage game and leapt out on deck. While Barry lashed the anchor, buoys, aluminum flagpole and buoy line together, she and Josh set the tubs at the base of the curved chute on the stern and began tying the ends of the skates together. At first she couldn't remember the knot, but then she purposely blurred her vision and let her hands work from memory. She nudged Josh. He glanced at it quickly and nodded approval.

"30 and 13," shouted Barry to the loudspeaker, so Jim could write the numbers painted on the neon yellow buoys into his log book.

"Whenever you're ready," Jim called.

"First end over," yelled Barry as he tossed the floats and played out the line until the anchor line was nearly taut, then tossed it over as well. With a measured clanging against the gunwales, stiff coils of line played out over the rail and sank out of sight. The tension transferred to the tubs of gear in the stern and, as Jim cruised at about half throttle along an edge visible only to him on the screen in the top house, 3,000 hooks disappeared faster than one could count over the top of the chute. Carla and Josh shoved fresh tubs aft and removed empty ones to a stack.

"Last skate," yelled Josh, and Barry readied himself to start paying out the other buoy set up.

"Running line over!" yelled Josh. The engine slowed.

"Anchor over," called Barry. As he heaved the buoys and aluminum flagpole clear of the boat he called out, "End over!"

"I'm going to set this next one right in the Wishbone, so it'll be 15 minutes or so until we're on the spot," came Jim's voice from on high.

"Roger," replied Barry, "Are we going to need another 300 on that one then?"

"Roger that." And the crew readied another set and then another, each running miles along the ocean floor. Then they would wait—six, eight, ten hours--while skates, dogfish, black cod, gray cod, red snapper, rough eye, convicts, idiots, and hopefully several hundred halibut tried to get something for nothing at their little longline diner at the bottom of the sea.

They hosed down the deck, washing fallen bait and soggy bits of bait boxes out the scuppers. They peeled out of their rain gear and stepped into the house, which should have smelled of evening grub. Barry and Josh looked at each other, then at Carla.

"Mostly the girls knock off early and make supper while we finish the gear," explained Josh.

She started to shake her head, then snorted and smiled instead. "Okay, I'll fry the potatoes, make some biscuits, and find some corn. Barry, you burn the steaks and Josh, you make a salad."

"A salad?" he repeated in disbelief."

"Yes, a salad. Go!"

By the time Jim had the boat anchored and the engine shut off, a fine dinner was on the galley table. The four of them ate in silence, except for Josh who asked repeatedly for more greens until the bowl was slicked clean.

Barry stood and slid his dishes into the sink. He tipped his wrist and looked at his watch.

"Gonna haul about 6, Boss?"

"Yeah, about then."

"Okay." And he disappeared into foc's'le. Josh likewise vanished, leaving Carla and Jim alone on opposite sides of the small table.

"Nice dinner," he said, leaning back.

She nodded noncommittal.

"Be a short night," he said, "I'll help you with the dishes."

She shook her head.

"Oh, come on, I don't mind."

"That's good," she said as she stood and slid her plate on top of the other two, "because I cooked."

Not looking back, she, too, disappeared into the foc's'le and chuckled softly to herself as the thrumming of the fresh water pump at the galley sink echoed through the belly of the boat.

By 4:30, they were all aware that the wind had picked up some during the night. It sang in the rigging and threw yipping chihuahuas

127

of wave tops against the steel hull even here in the harbor. But soon the engine's roar, the whine of the hydraulic pump, and the clanging of the incoming anchor chain drowned out every other noise.

Carla poured herself a cup of coffee and though she didn't usually eat breakfast herself, after taking a look at the cold Pop Tarts in the hands of the crew, she threw together a giant Spanish omelet on the top of the oil stove.

Jim's share she raised through the hole at the top of the ladder and left on the floor of the tophouse, like a peace offering at the entrance to a dragon's lair.

She leaned against the table as the boat began to buck into an unpleasant chop and spray hissed in a ragged rhythm against the galley windows. The westernmost points of land blurred into the mass and shrank as the curve of the earth swallowed them.

"The ocean changes so fast," she mused aloud.

"Especially out here," said Barry.

"We're going to be hauling in the trough, aren't we?"

He nodded with eyebrows raised in resignation.

"At least part of the time. I'm surprised at this wind. It wasn't in the forecast. But if it doesn't get any worse, if the swell doesn't build, with Jim at the roller, you'll hardly notice. That boy is smooth."

"Tell me about it," she mumbled.

They all took their positions as Jim drove up on the buoy. Barry reached out, hooked the line, and pulled the floatation assembly aboard. Josh threaded the line through the gurdy and began hauling it in. While 300 fathoms of buoy line coiled into waiting tubs, she watched Jim's back as he expertly judged wind, tide, and current, nudging the boat into and out of gear and flicking the pilot lever side to side to keep just the right amount of pressure on the incoming line which rolled popping and grinding through the sheaves. Gulls hovered effortlessly beside the boat as it rocked up and down in the chop. The gear anchor came over and she and Barry wrestled it into place while Jim untied its knots.

Again she waited, leaning against the hatch, entranced by the ballet of his hands as he judged each approaching hook, gaffing gray cod and tossing them unseen over his shoulder into the hold, gaffing red snapper and all their spiny cousins into a side checker to be bled and later filleted and even later delivered to the old timers in town whose knotted old knees had long since conceded victory to the sea. When dogfish with their alien eyes and ghostly pale skates came up, he let the guard horns on the roller wrench the hooks free. With a crystal splash, they returned to their own deep green reality.

Black cod and undersized halibut he shook free unharmed with a deft flick of his gaff. Halibut 32 inches and over he gaffed and held with both hands against the gurdy's inexorable pull. When the lighter weight gangion between the hook and the line snapped, he flipped the white bellied monsters into the checker beside him.

Carla shook her head as the fish began to pile up. A man who could keep so much in mind; wind and tide and depth and gear and bait and machinery and weather and current and specie and regulation and price and profit and crew and still keep his balance on a rolling deck was a marvel.

Was that why one woman wasn't ever enough?

As he slid another one into the checker he looked over his shoulder at her with his eyebrows raised.

"Do you remember what to do?" he asked.

She snorted with more certainty than she felt and picked up a heavy metal club. She hammered the fish right behind its ugly little green eyes, right where its brain should have been. Then she sank a gaff into its stunned and stiffly spasmed body and, slinging with her hips, got it onto the waist high hatch cover. She slid the knife around the gills, cut the diaphragm out and sliced from anus to chin, which even on a fish this size was less than eight inches. The entire assemblage of innards pulled out together and she heaved the pinkish mass over the rail behind her. A wave hit the side of the boat and she grabbed the hatch for balance. Jim peeked over his shoulder and smirked as he slid another fish into the checker, so she rammed her upper hand deep into the gut cavity and clawed out the fish's gonads. She flung the bloody balls just past his shoulder. He had turned away though and was watching the line with its deadly hooks slide over the stainless rollers. Gulls screeched and fought over the delicacies as they hit the water.

Carla took a scraper made from a loop of bandsaw blade fastened to a wooden handle and scraped the bloody bits that remained in the cavity, rinsed it in a cursory way, and slipped it into the opening in the hatch. Barry was beside her now, just finishing his own fish. He slid it over to her to rinse while he hefted four more out of the checker and clubbed each in preemptory self defense. They worked in steady rhythm, bracing against the hatch as the deck bucked under their feet. Her anger was soon spent in slicing, scraping, and ripping out intestines and gonads. At the end of each skate, she brought empty tubs to where Josh sat and wrestled the filled ones onto the shelves in the bait shed.

Halfway through the set, they shifted places and Barry took the roller, landing fish nearly as deftly as Jim, while Carla sat at the gurdy, resting her legs and back as she coiled the empty gear. Her hands were stiff and her face splattered with blood by the time they finished, but she went inside and made sandwiches for everyone as they ran to the end of the next set.

She heard them talking in the tophouse as she stood at the foot of the ladder.

"Best female crew you've ever hired," came Barry's voice.

"Best cook, too," offered Josh.

"And better looking to my mind than all those empty headed bimbos put together," growled Barry, "even though I know it's none of my business."

"You're damned right it isn't!" Jim shot back.

She gave the silence two seconds, just long enough that it was possible for her to have not heard, then popped head and shoulders up the hole with a plate of sandwiches.

"Thanks!" chorused Barry and Josh.

She smiled and disappeared before Jim was forced to say anything. She bounced off one side of the corridor then the other as she made her way aft. She beamed to herself as she battened down the galley to keep things from taking flight in case the sea got any steeper.

On the next set, she ended up in Barry's spot as he slid in to spell Josh, so she saw the snarl coming aboard at the same time Jim did. He slowed the gurdy and hovered over the ball of hooks, line, and twisted gangions. One gangion snapped and the whole mass jerked several feet backward toward the sea quicker than the eye could comprehend.

He stopped the gurdy, unwilling to send it through the machinery and endanger Barry.

"Hand me a strap. We'll tie it up and try to take some of the tension off," he called.

But as they both turned away, the snarl exploded in a storm of flying hooks. Jim raised an arm at the sound of the first snap and the hook headed for his face caught in his forearm instead. As the snarl unfolded, fathoms of it went back down into the water. The hook in Jim's arm jerked him against the side. He grabbed onto the roller and Carla watched in horror as the hook slid down his arm and came tight at his wrist.

She leaned far over the side and slashed the gangion that threatened to pull him through 300 fathoms of ice cold ocean. As he stood again, she saw blood running through the gash in his oilskins.

"Barry, we're on the last skate," he said evenly. "You take the roller. Josh, you man the gear. Take it easy and let's see if we can get this set wrapped up without any more mishaps."

Looking at Carla, he jerked his head toward the house and they ducked under the gear and went inside.

Under the oilskin jacket, there was no need to cut the shirt sleeve away. It lay open from elbow to wrist. It was his watch that had finally caught the hook and, pinned tight inside his glove, could not give way. The slice in his arm began just below the elbow and, except for a gouge in the meatiest part of his forearm, had done little more than part the skin.

"You got lucky there," she said with relief.

"Yeah, I'll say. Must be my lucky day."

"I just meant it could have been a whole lot worse."

"Thanks for cutting me loose. I was just about to go over. I'm surprised you didn't let me drown."

She said nothing and didn't hazard a look at his face.

"Take the shirt off. We'll get this cleaned up. You may need stitches."

"I don't have time for stitches. Just get the peroxide out and wrap it up."

She scrubbed it without mercy, blood poisoning from the multitude of nasty bacteria in and on fish being the primary danger in a hook wound. He clenched his teeth and screwed his face hard to one side when she poured hydrogen peroxide into the gash. When the bubbling subsided she wiped the foam away and doused it again. Then they filled it full of triple antibiotic cream, pulled the worst of it together with band aids and electrical tape and wrapped it, elbow to wrist in clean cotton.

"Thanks," he said as he gingerly pulled a clean shirt up over the arm.

"It'll hold you until we get town," she said.

"I'll probably have you change it all again tomorrow, if you don't mind."

"We're not going to town tonight?"

"Hell, no. We've still got over 20,000 pounds to catch. We'll go to town when we're done."

"Jim," she said incredulous, "you need stitches!"

"Carla," he said bitterly, "I don't need you to tell me how to run this part of my business. I may not be a neat freak or a numbers freak or a walking calculator or a complete control freak like you, but I know what I'm doing out here."

The door burst open and Barry and Josh tumbled in.

"How's the arm, Boss?"

Jim inhaled sharply and turned toward the crew. "Good as new," he said. "Everything squared away on deck?"

"Yup. We gonna haul that other set tonight?"

"Might as well." He turned and headed for the ladder to the tophouse. "Be about an hour, maybe an hour and a half before we're on the spot. Maybe we could get an early dinner out of the way, then haul, and hit the sack before midnight."

Carla stripped out of her oilskins and silently began dinner preparations. She was stunned and deeply bruised and felt suddenly unsure of the shape of the chasm that lay between them.

Landing Black Cod

Shifting Halibut to the Hatch for Dressing

135

Offloading Barndoor Halibut

"Starvin' to death. Starvin'! J-14 is a real desert and J-12 is worse." Warren Olsen's whine was shot through with glee and static. Steve recognized the numbers from their code sheet. J-14 was practically at the other end of the grounds from where he was and while 'starving' was their code for heavy duty fishing, starving was the genuine adjective for the poor catch at his own end of the world.

"Don't matter how fancy of electronics you got when the fishin's this poor," Warren went on, "but you gotta love this computer. At least you can watch yourself starve to death in style."

"Right," replied Steve, "I'll have to take a look at it when we get back to town. Be a long time before I can afford anything like that with the way this season's going. Anyway, thanks for the shout. That's all I got. I'll be out."

Steve hung the microphone back on its metal tines. His eyes combed the horizon beyond the point and studied the speed of the clouds at every altitude. He switched the radio to the weather station and let the computer generated voice roll through its identification and several minutes of unhelpful statistics while he studied the chart and measured distance and therefore time between his location and his coding buddy up the coast.

"Winds variable to 15 knots, becoming southeast to 20 knots. Seas to building to 5 feet. Outlook, southeast winds to 20 knots seas to 5 feet," droned the robot.

Steve refolded his chart, switched back to channel 16 and walked to the back deck. As he pulled on his gloves, he surveyed the empty fish checkers Holli had long since rinsed clean.

"Let's pull the gear," he said as he jumped into the pit. "They're really getting 'em up at the Cape. Forecast is just good enough, I think we can sneak up the outside coast and be there by midnight. If we run up the inside it will take us until tomorrow afternoon to get there and we'll miss two full tide changes. Okay by you?"

"You're the captain," she said with smile and a small nod of her head. She pushed her gurdy in gear and turned to wait for the first snubber to break the checkered surface. Steve changed course toward the black tumble of boulders that lay between them and the open ocean. If it got too bad they could always turn around and buck back in behind the point, he thought. It might be a little rolly, but they should have it on their stern most of the way. Maybe this little bit of wind was the 20 southeast they had forecast for later. And in that case, they could certainly handle five foot seas without any problem.

When they first cleared the point, conditions were manageable. Riding high on a following sea, they made good time, but within a couple of hours, manageable had become marginal. A wind still far off shore had gathered up a series of huge lumps and was pushing them up the coast against their stern.

Disappointed, wordless, with his jawed squared against an uncaring ocean, Steve began to angle in toward the nearest harbor. They wouldn't make it to the hot fishing today and might have to wait out the weather for who knows how long before they could sneak back inside into protected waters.

The new course put the rolling seas on their stern quarter and the autopilot could no longer keep the boat from leaning sharply and shearing off course as the lumbering swells caught up to them. He steered by hand, countering each tremendous surge a half second in advance.

Holli watched from the galley table as he fought to keep the boat on an even keel. The immensity of the surging seascape awed her. When the crests of the jade hills passed beside the galley windows,

138

the late afternoon sun shone through them and their translucence emphasized their depth. In her mind the sea instantly transformed from a sparkling surface on which they rode and rolled to an impossibly huge universe of water, stretching further than she could see in several directions; west, north, south, and down. She pictured their tiny boat bobbing on top of the 2000 feet of water beneath them and felt her heart tighten around her windpipe.

She grasped the edge of the table as the boat dipped between two waves. Then suddenly the engine began to race rhythmically, revving to full throttle, nearly choking, then revving, choking, again, again, and again.

"Fuel filters!" he shouted as he dove for the engine room. "Take the wheel!"

"What?" she called, scrambling up from the table.

"The rolling stirs up sediment in the fuel tanks. Blocks the filters. Take me a minute to clear it. Wish we had those spare filters, but I think I can fix it. Try to keep her stern to." And he disappeared beneath her feet.

The *Edna Mae* rose like a majestic duck as the next swell rolled under her stern. Holli was lifted onto her toes and waited for the broach on the other side. She leaned into the wheel to counter it. The rudder telegraphed the vibrating strain against the force of the roll all the way through the linkages into her fingers clamped tightly around the spokes of the wheel. The curling wave hissed along the sides of the boat. Silvery baubles of foam were nearly level with her eyes as they were pushed forward along the crest of the heaving sea. Again the shudder from the steering rattled the wheel, but she held it on course.

The galloping engine gradually steadied and Holli released a deep breath. Then it coughed violently, caught briefly, coughed again, and died. Silence folded around her like a shroud. She felt the stern rise once more, but without momentum of her own, she could not counter the ocean's whims.

When the crest passed midships, the boat teetered as on a mountain top then broached sideways into the trough. As it slid sickeningly to starboard, Holli held onto the wheel, whose only use now was as an anchor to keep her from flying against the side of the house. Each wave after that threw the boat violently one way then the other, dipping the rails to their very edges in the boisterous swells.

Then, as sometimes happens, the wind and tide conspired to pile two already large waves on top of each other. The colossus rose over the stern quarter of the helpless boat and Holli turned when she felt its shadow cover her.

"Steve!" she screamed, as a hundred tons of green water thundered onto the deck, shunting the whole boat sideways and buckling the wall of the house as it smashed forward. Inside it darkened to deep green and the galley windows cracked under the pressure. When they rose up toward the next crest, she caught a glimpse of their rubber raft tumbling past on the wave tops, its lines snapped and frayed. But before the decks could clear, a second monster hurled itself against the side of the house and the windows broke in a torrent of green water and glass that rushed around her feet and spilled down into the engine room.

"Steve!" Holli yelled, "Steve!"

She clung to the wheel as water sloshed around her legs. Another wave splintered against the hull, shoving the boat onto its beam ends. It wallowed heavily, lower in the water with each wave that poured through the gaping frame and filled the belly of the boat.

"Steve!" she yelled again.

His head, streaked with black grease, broke the oily surface, and with his first gasp he called, "Get the survival suits!"

"The what?"

"The Gumby suits! Get up on top of the house and get the Gumby suits! I gotta go back down and shut off the tanks." He dove before she could scream.

She climbed the ladder and flipped open the hatch to the bridge. On her hands and knees she crawled over to the storage box and pulled out two orange rubberized bags. Glancing quickly around she saw the deck was awash and Steve was on it. He yelled into a pocket sized radio. She heard, "Mayday, mayday, mayday. Fishing vessel Edna Mae. White hull, blue house. We're going down two miles west of Banshee Point. Mayday, mayday, 2 miles west of Banshee Point."

He climbed the outside ladder to the bridge with one hand, yelling his mayday as he came.

"Come on! Shake 'em out and get 'em on!"

She unsnapped the case and shook the first suit out. It unrolled at their feet. She unsnapped the second one and a sleeping bag hit the deck. A note fluttered in the wind and Steve caught it in his fist. 'Borrowed your suit for a hunting trip but left this as collateral. Have it back 2 weeks at the latest— Jack'.

"Son of a bitch," Steve growled. He wrinkled the note and flung it away. "Put on the suit!"

"What about you?" she countered, looking around for the nearest land.

It was in sight, but much further than either of them could swim unprotected. She knew survival time in these frigid waters was five minutes or less.

"Put it on!" he yelled.

She lay down on the suit, kicking one foot then the other into the huge legs. He grabbed the life ring and tied it to a loop on the suit. She gathered great folds of material around her elbows as she wiggled her hands toward the big mitts at the ends of the suit's arms.

"What about you?" she asked again. The only sound was the water hissing around the boat and tools and tackle clunking against its sides and top.

"Son of a goddam bitch," he said quietly, his teeth clenched. He checked the light attached to the suit pocket and pulled the whistle free. "It's all we've got," he said. "Take it off."

Holli's eyes only grew wider and she stared at him in disbelief.

"Get out of the suit."

A wave hit the side of the house and tilted the deck beneath them until they both nearly slid off. It did not right itself.

"Take it off!" His voice was urgent.

She slid out of the suit and, bracing herself against the now useless wheel, she watched silently as he pulled the lifesaving neoprene around himself.

"I don't know if anyone heard us," he said as he tucked his hair inside the hood. "I don't even know if this thing was transmitting." He braced himself against the box as the boat listed further to starboard. Angry tears filled Holli's eyes when she saw him reach for the two sides of the zipper.

"Hurry," he said, "climb in."

"What?" she blinked.

"Climb in. Here." He held out the sides of the suit and waited for her to step in. "Spoons," he said, "Come on!"

She pulled herself over and backed up to him, stuffing one leg down inside with his. He held her around the waist as she fought to get the other leg in.

"Here! Put this on." He bent into the box and pulled out a fleece hat with ear flaps and a chin strap. She didn't argue the fashion statement. She pushed her hair up inside and jammed the hat down, snapping it in place.

"Can you get the zipper?" he asked.

She tucked in loose clothes, pressed herself close against him and was able to tug the zipper halfway up her chest. She slipped one arm inside the sleeve with his.

"Hand me the radio again."

She reached out with her free arm and picked up the radio. He struggled to get an arm loose and finally said, "Hell, you keep trying."

She held the radio close to her mouth, thought about her parents and her brother, the broad starry nights and unshifting hills of Idaho. She called into the gathering darkness, "Mayday, mayday. Fishing vessel Edna Mae, white hull, blue house, going down two miles west of Banshee Point. Repeat two miles west of Banshee Point. We are dead in the water and sinking."

Her voice broke and she began to sob. He brought his arms around her waist and tucked his head into the crook of her neck.

"We'll be okay, Holli. Shhh...we'll be okay. We won't leave the boat until we have to. It'll be easier for them to see it than us." But at that point the water rose around their ankles and the last of the air escaped out the pilot house windows in great lazy bubbles the size of dinner plates. Holli tucked the radio and her arm inside and tugged the zipper of the suit as high as it would go. They sat backwards into the water and struck out for Banshee Point, pulling a steady backstroke in forced unison.

They were too buoyant to make much real headway toward shore, but not so buoyant that they rose above the cresting waves. Each one bubbled over Holli to some depth, pouring breathtakingly cold water into the unzipped breach. She felt icy streams of it run along her torso and down into the cavities between herself and Steve. She gasped with the first one and then just clenched her teeth in anticipation of the next. The water stung her eyes and she was amazed anew at how salty it was. She coughed and spat and tried to lift and turn her head when she saw a big one coming. Then she remembered Steve beneath her.

"Are you okay?" She tried to twist to see him.

"I'm fucking drowning!" he sputtered.

He had stopped paddling and now fumbled blindly along her chest. He patted her breast and she flinched.

"Sorry," he mumbled and she smiled in spite of herself.

"What are you looking for?" she asked.

"A hose. We need to blow up the ring. There's a little black hose with a stainless fitting on the end."

"Got it," she said and pulled their right arms over to where the hose lay beside the zipper.

"Blow it up. Quick. Press the end down with your teeth and blow."

She fumbled the hose toward her face and snagged the end with her teeth. The metal bit into her gums when she pressed it down, but she blew and blew until she felt the ring inflate. It brought Steve's head out of the water and, as there was still some air trapped in their legs, they sat V shaped, most of the open zipper above the water between dowsings.

"Better," he said and started stroking again, but Holli found that at each peak, the wind caught them and sucked away what little warmth remained in her water soaked clothes. Her nose, lips and cheeks were soon numb and she felt the icy teeth of the wind tear the life from her chest with every blast.

As they rose on the crest of a particularly high wave, she craned her head frantically toward shore. Banshee Point was a speck of black rock visible only for the crash of breakers that bathed it in phosphorescent foam.

Then the sea folded up around them again and they were in alone in a slick valley of glassy green. At the head of the valley, Holli saw the sky begin to color. Night was near.

Dwayne Dickson had heard the loud hum of a radio transmitting on low batteries. He heard it twice and knew from the lack of static that it was nearby. He switched on a radio direction finder, generally used to pinpoint someone's supposedly secret report to his buddy about how many fish he had or hadn't caught. Now he hunkered down before it, hoping the radio would broadcast again and watching the red lights flicker each time his other radio caught a signal.

When the hum came over the set again, the bleep steadied at 230 degrees. Dwayne rose to scan the horizon at 230 degrees.

"Not much out there. Open ocean all the way to Japan."

He studied the lights again as the hum filled his pilothouse. Probably nothing, he thought, but if someone was in trouble, it could be big trouble.

Out on deck he eyed the ocean beyond the point as he eased himself into the cockpit. He pushed the gurdy in gear and scanned he horizon right to left, left to right as he waited for the gear to break the surface. He knew by the spray of white against the jagged silhouette as well as the diminished swell that rocked his heavy wooden troller even this far up the protected channel, that the ocean was restless tonight.

"I guess I've been wanting to have a look out there anyway," he said as he began dropping gear into neat coils on the stern, "I just didn't know it." He cleaned his fish, slipped them into the hold and covered them with a shovelful of ice. Then he turned the bow of the *Grey Lady* to a new heading, 230 degrees, and ran the throttle up to 1650 rpm.

Steve stayed warm enough. Holli's body protected him from the wind and his own steady strokes even fueled a mild sweat. Holli however soon dropped into the haze of near hypothermia. He noticed when her arms stopped pumping with his and he spoke to her.

"Come on, Holli. Come on, Holli girl. We're almost there. Just a little further. You can do it. Pump it, girl. Come on, help me, Holli."

He heard her whimper but felt no response in her arms or legs. He bent forward and felt the side of her neck with his cheek. It was very cold.

"Talk to me, Holli. Talk to me. Are you cold? How cold are you?"

"I'm so cold," came her answer, barely audible in the vast, screaming darkness.

"What do you want, Holli? How about some hot chocolate? Would you like that?"

"No."

"A sauna," he said, stroking harder, "wouldn't a steamy, hot sauna be nice? Would you like that, Holli?"

"Yes," she whispered.

"Help me, Holli. Get me to shore and I'll find you a sauna. I promise, Holli. Pull! Pull with me! Pull!"

He swam in a panic, heartened when he felt her arms move a little against his.

"That's it. Pull with me. Stay with me, Holli. Stay with me." He leaned forward again and pressed his lips to her neck.

She rolled her head against his and whispered toward his ear, "I can't, Steve. I can't. I'm so cold."

"No you don't, Holl! You stay with me. Pull with me. Pull." There was no response. "Pull!" he shouted. "Pull! God damn it! Pull!"

146

In the dark, Dwayne could smell the diesel before he could see it. Driving in circles with his spotlight, he found what he thought was the epicenter.

Oily rainbows, fractured by the turbulent seas, rose to the surface all around him. Swiveling his spotlight downwind, he looked for a flotsam trail and saw a darker splotch just below the heaving surface. As it rose into sight on the crest of the next wave, Dwayne steered the bow toward it. He ran outside and picked up a long handled gaff from the cockpit. He hung onto the rigging and swung far out over the water, catching the edge of the mass in a one handed sweep and dragging it onto the deck. It was a sleeping bag and, as he ran it through his hands, he saw in black marker across the edge large child like letters that spelled out the name 'Jack Trimble.'

"Well, I'll be damned."

He dropped the bag and went back inside, his searchlight slowly taking stock of the nearby debris. He plucked the radio mike from its prongs.

"Hello the Scout...the fishing vessel Scout. Grey Lady WXK 4547, calling the Scout. Got it on, Jack?"

His eyebrows drew together as he waited for a reply he was sure wasn't coming. He tried one more time.

"Calling the Scout...the Scout. Grey Lady WXK 4547 calling the Scout."

He scratched the stubble on his chin with the head of the mike while he held the stern into the wind and was pushed along the trail of floating debris. Two matching Tupperware bowls and a woman's hairbrush wobbled beside him and tumbled down the face of the near vertical swell. Dwayne shook his head and said to himself, "This wasn't Jack's boat."

He clicked the mike impatiently. "Grey Lady clear the Scout. No contact."

He immediately switched channels and hailed the marine operator. He placed a ship to shore call to the one foul weather port he knew Jack Trimble favored.

"Pioneer Bar," answered a rough, disinterested voice.

"Hello. I'm calling from the grounds and this is kind of important, so can you take a look around and tell me if Jack Trimble is there? You might check under the tables, too."

"Yeah, he's here. Hang on."

Dwayne could hear glasses clinking, parts of several conversations and even the crack of pool balls as he waited for Jack to navigate to the phone.

"Hello?" came the thick voice.

"Jack? Jack Trimble? This is Dwayne Dickson."

"Hi ya, Dwayne, you son of a gun. How are you? Hey Pokey! It's Dwayne."

"I'm fine, Jack. Say, how long have you been in Sitka?"

"Aahh...I don't know, Dwayne. I'd hafta think. Couple a weeks, I guess. I been waitin' for the ocean to lay down. It's rougher'n a cob out there."

"Sounds like it's pretty rough right there."

"Yup. It's been seasick in here all day. I think ol' Diego's gonna hurl. Hey! Watch the shoes, man!"

"Jack?"

"Yeah? He just missed my shoes, man."

"Jack? I've got a question for you and I want you to think very carefully about it, okay?"

"Okay, Dwayne, you old son of a gun."

"Jack, can you think of any reason why your sleeping bag would be floating around out here off lower Baranof?"

"My sleeping bag? My blue one? I thought it was in my bunk. It was in my bunk last night. Or maybe the night before. I don't think I made it to my bunk last night."

"No, Jack, this one's red."

"Red? Ah, heck. My red one? Ah, heck. Dagone. I forgot. I'll bet he's pissed."

"Who's pissed, Jack?"

"Ol' Stevie. I traded him last fall so I could use his survival suit. I kinda forgot to tell him. And I kinda forgot to trade him back. Jees, I'll bet he's mad."

"Stevie Esterhaus?"

"Yeah, Esterhaus. I'll bet he's steamed."

There was a pause while a dim light dawned in Jack's fuzzy brain.

"Say," he slurred, "how come my sleeping bag's in the water. What did he do to my sleeping bag? It's probably ruined now. You find him, you tell him he owes me a new sleeping bag."

"Right, Jack," said Dwayne, "If I find him, that's the first thing I'm gonna tell him."

A gradual change in the sea and a building roar in his ears wakened Steve from his mechanical stroking. He noticed an upwelling current that raised him higher onto each crest. The swells grew sharper and steeper. They curled, broke, and foamed all around him. There was a tremendous crashing behind his head and he tried to get a look at the shore they were going to land on. All he saw was the creamy chaos of breakers and the blackness of the land above them. He curled his arms around Holli and closed his eyes as a wave threw them landward. They were tumbled and flung against the rocky slope. Steve gasped for air and took a desperate purchase on a pocked boulder they had just missed smashing into.

As the water sucked back down past his waist, he stumbled to his feet and fought toward higher ground. The water in the suit weighed him down so that his legs buckled, sending them into the tumbling brine again and again. The next big roller clipped him in the knees and threw him face down on top of Holli. She didn't move. Frantically he rolled off her and pushed himself up. He grabbed her around the waist like a rag doll and lumbered steadily toward the alder fringe. He sank onto the mat of last winter's beach grass. His breath rasped in this throat, already raw from mouthfuls of sandy salt water and nearly swollen shut with fear.

He did not call her name but found the zipper and fought one arm free. He laid his big square fingers on her neck. He thought there was a pulse. He then laid his hand on her upper lip but could not tell if it was her breath or the wind that cooled his skin.

As carefully as he could, he pulled her out of the suit and laid her behind a drift log partially sheltered from the wind. He quickly pulled the suit off, emptied gallons of water out of it and gently tucked her limp body back inside, pulling the zipper up to her chin. He checked again for a pulse and quietly tested the air with her name.

He unfastened the strobe light from the suit and rapped it with his knuckles, but it had been smashed in one of their falls. Instead he pulled a tiny flashlight out of the suit's pocket, picked up a long tapered rock, and fought his way through the alder fringe into the forest.

His feet soon found the deer trail and he followed it, flashing his light on every tree he passed. He came at last to a tree that lay across the path which, in its falling, had scarred a neighbor. That neighbor had bled a scab over the wound and it was this crystallized covering and the soft wood around it that he attacked with his crude hammer. Chunks of wood and pitch fell at his feet and when he had all he could carry in two hands, he gathered them and ran back along the forest track.

He dropped them on the stones in front of her and dashed back into the trees. This time he shone his light upward and broke off dead twigs and small branches that still hung on the lower trunks of the giant spruce trees. Digging once more into the pocket of the suit, he found the lighters still in thin store plastic. He tore one out and struck a flame against his precious store of pitch and tinder. He crouched low over the growing flames to shield them from the unpredictable gusting of the wind.

So intent was he on his fire, so low behind the drift log, that he did not see the flashes from the spotlight on the *Grey Lady* as it rose briefly on the distant swells, moving west to east and finally vanishing around Banshee Point.

Dwayne pulled his mike from its holder just as the radio broke squelch.

"Pan, pan. Pan, pan. Pan, pan. This is United States Coast Guard Juneau Communication Center, United States Coast Guard Juneau Communication Center. Time: Alaska Standard Time 21:03. An EPIRB signal has been picked up by satellite in the vicinity of southern Baranof Island. All vessels in the area are advised to keep a sharp lookout, assist if possible, and notify Coast Guard Juneau Communication Center. This is United States Coast Guard Juneau Communication Center out."

Dwayne paused a moment to let the air clear.

"Calling the Emerald Sea. Grey Lady, WXK 4547. Emerald Sea. You still got it on, Jim?"

The violent rocking diminished as the point shielded the *Grey Lady* from the worst of the wind. Inside the point, the reflection of the waves off the rocks created a jagged sea on top of the ocean swell.

"Yeah, Dwayne. Go 10?"

"Roger, 10."

Both men switched away from the hailing frequency to the quieter intervessel channel.

"Get me here, Dwayne?"

"Gotcha fine, Jim. Did you hear that pan pan?"

"Yeah, I heard it. You got any idea who it is?"

"I got a pretty good idea. I think the *Edna Mae* went down out here off Banshee Point. I just can't figure out what he would have doing clear out here in this slop. I was wondering if you saw him anywhere out here today."

"Jeez! No, huh uh. Didn't see him today. I saw him as we were coming out yesterday, but he was way up inside. It was too rough for a boat his size out here. Hell, it's too rough for us. This southeast sure came up fast. We just pulled the last skate and we were going to hole up till it lays down a little, but if you think Stevie's gone down somewhere out here, we'll sure help you look."

"Roger that. Something went down out here, that much is for sure." Dwayne paused with the mike still on. He checked the fathometer and his chart, then peered out the black squares of window once again. "I'm not for certain sure, Jim," he said, "but I think I saw a flash of something on the beach. I'm going in behind Aldered Point and I'm going to try to take the skiff in. I just wanted to let someone know what was up."

"No kiddin'! We'll turn around and swing over that way."

"Roger. I'll hang on 10. I'm going to drop the hook now. I'll talk to you later."

"Okay. Keep us posted. We're on our way."

Dwayne let his mike dangle by its cord while he studied the chart for the best possible holding bottom. The radio crackled above his head once again.

"Dwayne, you still there? This is Mack."

"Roger, Mack. Got you loud and clear."

"Just wanted you to know, Kathy heard Stevie talking to his coding buddies up by the Cape earlier today. Sounded like they were hammering the kings and Stevie wasn't. She thinks he was going to head up there this afternoon."

Dwayne nodded. That would make sense. This blow wasn't in the forecast. "Well, thanks, Mack. I'm going to have a look. I'll let you know what I find."

"Roger. We'll head down that way. There's no fish up here anyway. I'll be out."

Dwayne dropped the anchor in the stickiest mud he could find and sat back hard on it. When he lowered his skiff into the water, it bobbed and bounced like a toy. The swells bathed the rocky shore in white and only by ducking inside a ragged finger of rock, did he avoid being thrown against the boulders. He dragged the skiff completely out of reach of the hungry waves and tied it to a beach alder. Then he struck out along the high tide line, picking his way with a flashlight to where he thought he had seen a flicker of fire.

"Don't do this, Holli," pleaded Steve in a hoarse whisper. He held her on his lap facing the fire, as close as they could sit with the flames now being thrown in every direction. He shivered as he clutched the dripping suit with her small body inside. His own clothes still pulled warmth from his skin as the wind whistled around them. He had cheered her on when her stomach had emptied a pool of salt water, but her eyes had never opened and her pulse remained weak and slow.

"How could I have done it?" he asked the darkness. "How could I have gambled your life against a few stinking fish?" He rocked her like a small child and felt hot tears run down his cheeks. "Don't leave me, Holli. Please."

153

He brushed his own tears from her face and saw her cheek was beginning to purple under the scratches from the rocky landing.

"I didn't ever mean to hurt you," he whispered. "Never." He shook his head and swallowed hard. "Do you know I wake up early every morning just to watch you sleep? You're so beautiful." He brushed a strand of matted hair from her cheek then stroked her face gently with the backs of his fingers. "I've been afraid to touch you. When I just look at you it feels like my heart's in a vise. When you smile it's like the sun comes out. You're the sun and the moon..." He shook his head. "You're everything. Please, don't go."

He squeezed his eyes tight shut then blinked up at the inky sky. Sniffing and shivering, he turned the radio at his feet to dry out another side of it. Then, gently, he laid her down. He went to the other side, the exposed ocean side, of the drift log and stacked a circle of rocks for a signal fire. Then he dove into the forest again to find dry wood for both fires.

When he finally turned back, carrying a double armload of wood, he panicked momentarily. He had lost sight of the fire. It wouldn't have gone out, he thought. Then he saw a flight of sparks and realized something was between him and the fire. Something big. Something leaning over Holli. He dropped his load of wood and picked up the longest, strongest stick in it. He let out a terrible scream, hoping to frighten the bear away. It turned and stood on its hind legs. Steve began to swing his limb and slash at the branches around him as he ran toward it. The bear stood taller and swayed side to side. Then it flashed a halogen light at him.

"Stevie?" it said.

Steve dropped the stick and ran to the fire. Dwayne shone the light up into his own face.

"Dwayne! You scared the crap out of me. How did you find us? Where are you anchored?"

154

"Sorry. Never mind. And not far from here. Are you okay? And how is she?"

"Jesus! I don't know. She's breathing and all, but she won't open her eyes."

"The skiff is less than a mile from here. Shall I carry her?"

"No. I will. You lead the way."

Dwayne kicked the fire out while Steve scooped Holli up, floppy neoprene arms and legs dangling loose. Dwayne shone one light ahead and one light behind himself as they picked their way across the rocky headland and onto the pocket beach where the skiff lay.

Steve gently lowered Holli onto the plank seat and ran to tear the bowline free. Together they launched the skiff on an incoming swell and Dwayne kicked the outboard into high speed reverse as Steve scrambled over the bow. They took a lot of spray and Steve shielded Holli's face with his body, the pelting salt water running down his back.

Dwayne cut the throttle and eased up to the leeward side of the *Grey Lady*. Steve reached up and made the bow fast and Dwayne the stern, but the two boats rode the waves so differently that the lines came taut, went slack, and jerked the skiff dangerously beneath their feet. Steve grabbed the rail of the big boat and vaulted onto the deck then lifted Holli from Dwayne's arms on the next upward swell. He carried her into the pilot house and lay her on the floor. Then he ran back outside to help Dwayne muscle the skiff aboard and tie it down.

While the older man hauled the anchor, Steve hovered over Holli, gently pulling her hair out of the sticky rubber hood and calling her name over and over. Dwayne stepped inside and slid the door closed behind him. He throttled up and headed into deeper water.

"How is she, do you think?" he asked.

"I don't know. I think she tries to open her eyes, but never quite can. I don't know what to do. Should we get the Coast Guard out here with a chopper?"

Dwayne pointed to the cubby like stateroom. "Best thing to do right now is lay her in that bunk. Take those wet clothes off. Yours, too. And get both of you into a sleeping bag. There's two of them. Unzip the second one and put it on top. Warm her up with your own body heat. As soon as I get around the corner and out of this swell, I'll make a fresh pot of coffee. Go. Now! Get her out of that wet sponge."

Steve left the soaking shell of the survival suit on the floor of the cabin and took Holli into the stateroom, closing the door behind him. Dwayne meanwhile called Jim on the *Emerald Sea* and let him know the survivors were safe. He called Mack Harrison and asked that they meet and transfer Holli and Steve to Harrison's high speed gillnetter. It would shave a couple of hours off the running time to town.

Forty minutes later, with the boat on auto pilot and in the lee, Dwayne tapped on the stateroom door and brought in a cup of fresh coffee. The small room was like the promised sauna, steam rising from both of their bodies. Holli's head rested on Steve's gently rising and falling chest. She lifted her eyes and demurely pulled a corner of the sleeping bag over the tops of her creamy breasts. A rising blush in her cheeks attested to healthy circulation. It was Steve who slept like a dead man, partly buried under the tangled curtain of Holli's hair.

Dwayne offered the cup as he fought to control the corners of his mouth.

Holli shook her head.

He cleared his throat and said, "Looks like you're fully recovered. Is he okay?"

"Yes, sir," she nodded and smiled, "he certainly is."

Dwayne closed the door behind him and settled into the pilot's chair for the long ride into town.

"Mack, you still on 10?"

"Roger, Dwayne, we're at full throttle and headed your way."

"Well, thanks anyway, but looks like these two kids are gonna be fine. And I don't think they're gonna mind the extra couple of hours of running time."

"Ah, that's great, Dwayne. Glad to hear it. If you're sure you don't need us, we'll turn around and get some shut eye."

Dwayne sipped his coffee and smiled out the black windows into the night.

"I'm sure," he said. "Thanks. I'll be out."

Marie skittered down the steep ramp and crammed her hands deep into her pockets. The gray mist of morning had not yet been pierced by full sun. A glow on the island tree tops to the west marked its slow climb up the icy mountain ridges behind her. She huddled into her collar and hurried to join the small crowd gathered at the empty stall of the *Grey Lady*. Fingers pointed and necks craned as the boat cleared the last bend and turned to make for the harbor.

Dwayne had only asked that Myra meet them there with the car. Though Holli insisted she was fine, Steve was equally adamant that she be checked out at the hospital.

Myra had only called Steve's mother and Holli's cousin Marie, but the whole town knew one of several versions of the events by daybreak and a dozen of them were now comparing details and arguing story lines as the main players chugged toward them.

Steve tossed lines to waiting hands while Dwayne eased the boat into the slip.

"What are all these people doing here?" Holli asked Dwayne as she saw the flash from Arlen Pinkstad's camera.

"You know how a small town is. Mostly they want to be sure you're okay."

"I'm fine, for Pete's sake!"

"Not just you," said Dwayne gently, and Holli saw the sea of hands reaching for Steve's, chucking him on the shoulders and patting him on the back. His mother's hand stroked his cheek and Steve leaned over the rail to hug her and wipe away tears. Steve turned and held out a hand to help Holli over the high threshold. When she climbed out the galley door, elfin in Dwayne's jacket and her cheek in full purple bloom, Marie gasped. She jumped on board and pulled Holli into a fierce, protective hug. Steve's own outstretched arm fell to his side, robbed of its strength by Marie's unintentional rebuke.

"Marie," pleaded Holli, "I'm fine."

"Yeah, you look fine!" she snapped.

"Let's get her up to the hospital, just for a check up," said Steve and the crowd parted as he stepped onto the float. At the head of the finger, Gabriella Hanson blocked the way. Her dark Pacific island hair was now streaked with gray and her petite body gone nearly square. Arms crossed and feet wide, she would be dealt with. She jerked her head over her shoulder toward the *Stormy,* now in its second season of idleness, the hand lettered For Sale sign faded to watery gray in the front window.

"You take him," she said.

"Oh, Mrs. Hanson, I have a lot of things to sort out first. Thank you, but I can't..."

"Pah! He's a good boat and he needs to get out. You do me a favor to fish him till fall." She pulled a padlock key from the pocket of her red and black checked jacket and dropped it in his hand. Then she turned on her heel and walked away. Steve watched her lean forward to find her balance point at the base of the ramp.

"Oh!" she shouted and straightened back up. "He always backs to port," she explained with a wave of her left hand, "Not bad, but you gotta keep a eye on him. Port."

"Port," nodded Steve.

She nodded back, satisfied, and bent nearly double, trudged up the ramp.

Sandy Bergren and Neil Esterhaus passed her coming down and by the time they all met, the crowd had once again engulfed Steve, Holli, and Marie. Sandy smiled warmly.

"Nice to see you in one piece."

"Thanks," said Steve.

They both turned and looked at the proud plumb bow of the *Stormy*, one of the beefiest wooden boats for its size ever built.

"I heard she was going to let you fish it for the season. You probably need a thing or two to get it ready," mused Sandy, "but, hell! Take anything you need from the store and we'll settle up in the fall. Isn't that right, Neil?"

Neil, surprised by the sudden breach of store policy, hesitated for an ungracious instant. And in that half second, that tick of time in which his frigid soul flashed bare, he saw his world dissolve and reform. He watched the change in the eyes of every face. He felt the dock tilt as power shifted to the man beside him. In less than a heartbeat, months of calculation and cunning had evaporated to nothing. Even Pinkstad's eyes narrowed to piercing darts.

"Of course," he nodded toward his brother, speaking mechanically, knowing that in this town it probably wouldn't matter what he said ever again.

"Thanks," repeated Steve sheepishly, and after a handshake and much back slapping, the three moved away again, climbing single file up the sharply sloping ramp.

"Mr. Esterhaus?"

Steve jerked to a stop at the head of the ramp and Holli, intent on her own feet, bumped into him. He reached for her without taking his eyes from the man in front, while Marie steadied her from behind. Impatiently she shoved both of their hands away.

"Yes?"

159

"Lieutenant Stockton, U.S. Coast Guard. I have some questions for you, sir, about a possible oil spill. If you could come with me, please, we have some reports for you to fill out."

"Can't we do this later?"

"I'm afraid not, sir."

"I'll take her on up to the clinic," offered Marie. "Come on, Holl. My car's right here."

"Steve," began Holli, "I really don't..."

"Go on!" he said in a tone that made the lieutenant jump. Holli glared angrily and pulled Dwayne's jacket more tightly around herself. She stumped to the car, slammed the door and rode out of the parking lot without a backward glance.

EDITORIAL
by Arlen Pinkstad

"Over the years the sea has taken many fine men and women from us and the holes their passing leave in the fabric of our community can never be mended. We are grateful another such tragedy was averted this week."

Could he write great metaphors or what? Pinkstad's fingers paused above the keys as his eyes darted to a manuscript box moldering on the top shelf of his chaotic credenza. Someday he'd finish his novel and impress the pants off this whole town. The jerky second hand on the clock next to it caught his attention and forced out a hurried sigh. He furrowed his brow in concentration and leaned forward to reread his introduction.

The Esterhaus rescue filled two full pages with print and pictures. He was especially proud of the shot of Dwayne leaning on his arm out the pilothouse window, looking back at the crowd as it reached like a loving octopus to welcome back one of its own.

"...grateful another such tragedy was averted this week."

His eyes focused on a point far behind the surface of the screen, then jerked back as his fingers exploded in a blur of keystrokes.

"But one must ask, was everything done, is everything being done, to keep our men and women safe on the ocean, to minimize the dangers in this most dangerous of occupations?

We understand that the mechanical forecast was fully six hours behind on the latest weather data. Shouldn't current and accurate forecasting be paramount, especially here where so many lives depend on it?

We also understand that there was no Coast Guard helicopter launched in response to the *Edna Mae*'s EPIRB. What good does it do to require EPIRBs and to maintain an elaborate satellite system to monitor them if they don't result in saved lives?

Government agencies—and not just these two—have grown to the point where they are self perpetuating generators of obtuse forms and a never ending flood of regulations. And every new regulation spawns a regulator who, in turn, needs assistants and secretaries and underlings ad nauseum.

It is high time government was reminded that it was instituted to serve the governed and not the other way around. What we need is fewer regulations and more service, less meddling and more compassion, a government of the people and by the people, but first and foremost, FOR the people."

Arlen hit Save with a satisfied click. He read it through once more and nodded sharply. He decided it put just enough distance between himself and Neil's IFQ proposals without being a direct contradiction of the editorial stand he had taken three weeks ago. In the short time since the Esterhaus rescue and Neil's unmasking on the dock, conversations in the coffee shop and elsewhere around town had already pronounced those proposals dead and buried. Arlen had stuck his proverbial neck out and was grateful to have it back in one piece.

Suddenly he became aware of Darlene reading the screen over his shoulder.

"You write that all by yourself?" she asked.

"Of course I did," he huffed.

She turned away and poured him a cup of coffee.

"It's pretty good," she said, bringing the coffee to his desk. "You just might turn out to be a real newspaperman yet."

She smiled, poured herself a cup and disappeared back into the press room.

Arlen stared at the empty doorway for a long time.

Carla had wheel watch 3 AM to 6 on the run back to town. Alone in the tophouse, she found herself midwife to the morning. As she watched a young sun bloody the eastern sky, she felt she held a stake in the new day, that somehow, because she had had a hand in its coming, she should also have a say in its course. Did that make her a control freak?

The sun began to gild the tips of the dark spruce trees, brushing the early mist away with a golden broom. The mountain tops above blushed like proud breasts draped in snowy lace. Surely she wasn't wrong to resent Jim's chasing after every Jennifer, Trisha, and Heather in a double D cup. Surely. But she had to wonder if in treating him like a criminal she had created one. Alice Stimson hadn't been a threat to their marriage, but Carla knew that in her fear she had made it seem so. She had dug a protective trench and distanced herself from hurt and at the same time from the source of her joy. She seemed to herself now a withered and bitter woman, a creature of dust and gall. No wonder he sought pleasure elsewhere.

Gathering tears blurred the moire of indigo and lavender on the ocean's face. It became a slate wall, drear and infinite. Suddenly, the surface was broken as a lone cormorant slithered from the sea before the bow. She blinked and brushed her eyes clear. Like a snake raising its head to scout the terrain, the sleek black bird looked from side to side. It dove briefly then popped like a cork from the water. When the next wave crested beneath it, it thrust its serpentine head forward, stretched its wings, iridescent in the sharply slanting rays, and lifted into the air.

She followed its course, a black slash on the purple sea and did not hear or see Jim climb the stairs behind her.

"I'll take over," he said.

Carla started.

"Oh! You scared me. I didn't hear you come up."

He made a slow circle, checking the conditions in every direction as well as the lay of the boat.

"Seen much traffic?" he asked.

"No, it's been pretty quiet," she replied in a low voice.

She was reluctant to give up the helm. She made a minor adjustment to the autopilot and raised the brightness of the depth sounder to compensate for the daylight now streaming through the windows.

He sat on the day bunk behind her and crossed his long legs, propping his feet against the console to her left. He closed his eyes and they seemed to sink into the sockets of his skull.

"How's the arm?" she asked.

"It's kinda warm in spots," he said from behind closed lids. "Might have a little infection in there. I'll get some antibiotics when we get to town."

"Can I see it?"

"Sure."

She swiveled the chair around and stood. He held his arm out and she cautiously unwrapped the dressing. She slid a knife under the black bands of electrical tape and lifted the final layer of bandages off.

"Oh, Jim. It looks fevered." She twisted it gently to check the inside of his upper arm and he winced.

"I don't see any streaks. No blood poisoning, but it must hurt like hell."

"Oh, it's okay. Wrap it back up would you?"

"You know," she said, leaning close to smell the wound, "I think a hot pack might help. It'll draw more circulation to it and maybe kill any infection that might have gotten started. Mind if I try that?"

He shrugged.

"I'll be right back." She ducked down the stairs, found a clean towel, and wet it with water from the teakettle on the oil stove. She juggled it from hand to hand as she climbed back up into the tophouse. Jim lay on the bunk, eyes closed, arm angled away from his body. She folded the towel and laid it on his arm.

"Too hot?"

"Just right," he said. "You can get Barry up if you want to go to bed. He can stand my watch for me."

"No. I'm fine. For a while anyway."

She eased around his arm to where she could see the controls but did not sit back down in the pilot's seat. Instead she watched him. Four day's stubble and hair grown shaggy around the ears, mouth agape and clothes far from fresh, she still found he stirred an electric current in her physical core. It raced from deep in her pelvis to the base of her throat with a jolt that made her light headed. God, she loved him! Hesitantly, she reached out to stroke his forehead with the tips of her fingers.

He circled her wrist with the hand of his good arm. His lids opened on deep brown eyes throwing amber sparks. He pulled her down until her face was within an inch of his, then lifted his lips to barely brush hers. She pulled away, struggled to keep from falling into those eyes, from being seduced by those lips. And he let her go.

He closed his eyes again and Carla saw beads of pain at the corners.

"You can have it any way you want it," he said.

"What do you mean?"

"You're calling the shots. Just be sure this is the life you want."

Carla slid back into the pilot's chair. She scanned the horizon and saw before her an infinity of courses. Out here, and everywhere, the choices were uncountable and yet they always boiled down to two; do you cave in to fear or keep fighting it? Do you meet the world with courage and a vulnerable heart or hide from the hurt that might be out there?

She swiveled around to find him watching her. Slowly he raised himself on one elbow. His eyes were sharp, but his face was as open as a child's. "I'll do anything, Carla. But there's a price." He stood. He looked nowhere but into her eyes. "My price is all of you. All of you."

She turned the chair and lowered her feet to the floor. He took her hand gently. "And my price," she said, "is all of you."

His good arm went behind her neck and pulled her to him. Her hands slid around his waist and across the taut muscles of his back. They kissed tentatively, then with a desperate, grasping hunger. Abruptly, he let her go and turned to flip the trap door shut. He set the lock with his toe and turned once again toward her. She stepped to him and buried her face in the smell of his neck.

Suddenly she felt him stiffen against her and though his arms still held her, the embrace was mechanical. His chin thrust forward, its stubble pulling strands of her hair.

She craned her neck up as he rolled her to one side and picked up the binoculars. He focused them on a troller on the inside beach drag off their starboard bow. Carla looked, too, and recognized the *Bonnie Jean*, deaf Tony's boat. It was pointed bow to the beach and was much too close, even for this shallow drag. Then she noticed what Jim had.

"He's not moving," she said.

"He's not moving, but he's churning up a wake," he said without dropping the glasses. "His float lines are hanging straight down and his heavies have the bow poles bent almost to the water." He laid the binoculars on the dash and spun the *Emerald Sea*'s bow in toward the beach.

"He's stuck on that reef?" she asked.

"Get Barry and Josh up," replied Jim without looking at her. "And tell Barry to get that heavy tow line out of the lazarette. I don't think we're going to like what we find here."

Wordlessly Carla unlocked the trap door and slipped down the ladder. She shouted the deckhands awake then bundled herself against the early morning chill. She readied the tow line Barry handed her in big loops on the deck. All three hands stood at the rail as they drew nearer the old wooden shoe.

Jim pulled up to the stern of the *Bonnie Jean* slowly to keep the steel trolling lines out of his own wheel. He leaned out of the tophouse window, gradually forcing his bow in against the churning wash from Tony's prop. Barry jumped down onto the smaller vessel, ran the line through the aft hawsehole and made it fast to the biggest cleat he could find. From the deck, he pushed the throttle into neutral and the *Bonnie Jean* eased back until all her lines hung straight down.

Barry ducked into the low pilothouse and came back out moments later shaking his head. His lips were pursed tight under his great blonde moustache.

"Died at the galley table drinking coffee," he shouted up to them. "What do you want me to do?"

Jim looked down at Carla who was leaning over the rail below him. He said to her, "Pull that line tighter, can you? And throw Barry the forward tie up line. He pulled his head in and seconds later Josh tumbled out the door with wire cutters in his hands.

"I'll do it," she said, taking the snips from him. She jumped down onto the tarred wooden deck and slipped into the cockpit. She pulled and coiled the aft gear with practiced ease. She shook long dead fish, which cartwheeled stiffly to the bottom. She snipped off the two bow leads that had anchored the boat to the reef.

When she had the *Bonnie Jean* loose, and Barry had the poles hauled upright, Josh adjusted lines and buoy bags until the smaller boat was snugged firmly alongside the *Emerald Sea*. Carla went into the house and eased Tony's slumped body onto the galley bench. She brought a pillow and blanket from the fo'c'sle and covered him carefully. His eyes were closed and his skin already cold. She held his gnarled hand gently and kissed it before laying it across his chest. Then she pulled the kill wire on the engine and the *Bonnie Jean* rattled to stillness.

Jim was already backing away from the beach and Barry and Josh stood at the rail. He cut the engine as they helped her back onto the larger boat. She put the wire cutters away and went to stand beside Jim in the tophouse. His free arm held her close while the other steered them away from the rocks and into deeper water. She soaked up the warmth and strength of him as if filling a great void. Again and again he bent to kiss the top of her head.

Barry's dirty baseball cap appeared at the top of the stairs.

"Keep an eye on that boat," Jim barked, "Let me know instantly if we need more lines or need to move the ones we've got. And tell Josh to get on some breakfast."

"Right, Boss." Barry disappeared and they weren't disturbed again except for a plate of scrambled eggs and toast that slowly hardened unheeded beside their feet.

New Trolling Poles

Steve had the new trolling poles of the *Stormy* laid out across two empty stalls to work on the tips. He hammered fence post staples into the fresh wood. He attached foot long springs, bells, safety snubbers, and the tag lines that would eventually attach to the seven strand wire coiled on the new gurdy banks in the stern.

He reared back to drive the staple home, saw Holli out of the corner of his eye as she paused at the head of the ramp, and missed the pole on the downward swing. The hammer slipped from his hand as he fought to regain his balance, bounced off his shin, and, with an unforgiving plunk, sank into the bay.

He lowered himself carefully, teeth clenched, color rising, onto the rail on the edge of the float. It allowed him to watch her approach without pretending to do anything but rub the fast growing goose egg on his shin. They hadn't spoken since she had stormed off in Marie's car. Marie had called only to tell him that Holli was indeed all right.

He had a million things to say to her, how sorry he was for having endangered her life, how bad he felt about what had happened in Dwayne's stateroom, how good he felt about what had happened in Dwayne's stateroom, how much he loved her, how he wanted to make a life with her, how he couldn't imagine any kind of life without her, how beautiful she was, how incredibly good he felt just to see her again.

He took a deep breath, rose onto one leg and managed, "Hi."

She glanced up into his face, then at the *Stormy*, and then turned to look at the stall where she had expected to find the *Grey Lady*.

"I thought Dwayne might be here."

"Uh...he's over at the fuel dock."

"Oh." She raised the jacket that lay over her folded arms. "Maybe next time you see him, you could return this for me."

"Sure." He pulled the jacket off her arms and saw that she held an airline ticket in her hand. He could neither open nor close his mouth but breathed heavily through it like an injured animal.

She lifted the ticket as she lowered her head. Several eternities passed. Finally, she raised her eyes to his once more.

"Called my folks," she said. "They were pretty upset. Wired me this ticket to come home."

He closed his mouth, swallowed twice, and, hating himself, said, "So, you need a ride to the airport?"

She let the ticket fall and slap against her thigh. She turned on her heel and walked to the head of the finger float. There she paused, and he saw her shoulders heave and her head bow. He dropped the jacket on the dock but did not move.

She straightened, her back still to him.

"You know," she said, "my folks live in town now, but I was raised on a horse ranch and there's one thing my daddy taught me that I'll never forget."

"If a horse bucks you off, you gotta climb right back on?" he asked hopefully.

"No, but that's a good one, too. What Daddy told me was 'Never drink downstream from the herd.'"

Stevie's brow knit in puzzlement. He tried to find a thread of logic in that statement that he could hold on to, that would let him say the things he needed to say. Finally, he just shook his head and took a step toward her. He drew a deep breath, but just as he opened his mouth, she spoke again. Her words were a little wobbly and so quiet he barely heard them.

"I don't think I want to be anywhere near that herd again. I don't want to go back. Not to live. I like it here. I love it here, where there's enough room between people that you can see every one of them clearly, and care about them." She paused. "And care about them," she repeated softly.

He saw the logic now and a tentative smile broke over his face.

"Come here," he said gently. "Spoons."

He stepped forward as she backed up slowly, following true north on a deeply internal compass. His arms enfolded her into the warm harbor of his chest. He drew the honey brown hair away from one side of her face and kissed her neck lightly. "Mmmmmmmmm," he said, "Mmm, mmm, mmm."

Training up the next generation

The hall was packed. Hand knit and imported, sliver clasped sweaters in dizzying designs formed a woolen sea on the folding chairs. Not only was the town church too small for all of Tony's friends to bid him farewell, but an argument with the Lutheran pastor over a game of checkers 30 years ago made the Sons of Norway Hall the only logical choice for the funeral service.

Flowers filled the front, surrounding a gray plank with peeling black paint. The crooked letters spelled out 'TRAP No. 3', the sign from the fish trap Tony had manned before statehood. Another more recently painted board held a list of the boats Tony had crewed on or owned, beginning with a classic wooden halibut schooner out of Ballard and ending with the *Bonnie Jean*. There was a picture of Tony, too, as proud father or congratulatory uncle in a dark suit, very unlike the stooped and shuffling widower of more recent days.

Carla found it slow going up the aisle. Jim had words or a handshake for everyone within reach. At last they took seats next to Betty who had saved a few.

"It must have been awful for you," whispered Betty as the two hugged briefly.

"Not really," said Carla, "Just the way I'd like to go." She looked down the row past her cousin.

"Is that seat for Earl?" she asked, nicking her head down the row. "Is he here?"

Betty shrugged. "Haven't seen him."

"Is Neil coming?"

She shrugged again and picked up her purse from the empty seat beside her. Their gum smacking classmate who did reservations at the tiny airport leaned forward from the row behind them.

"Neil left on yesterday's southbound," she whispered. "Not a business trip either. Checked all the luggage we allow and then some."

Carla and Betty turned in unison and gave identical, not quite curt nods.

Carla leaned close to Betty's ear, "Don't you care?"

Betty whispered back, "One less mouth to feed," and shrugged again.

Tony's nephew, Billy, an old man himself, stood up from the front row and walked to the microphone. He opened the program in his hands to the eulogy inside. He stared at it for several minutes as the room hushed respectfully.

"I don't suppose there's more than half a dozen of us who can't read this for himself, so I don't see much point in me reading it to you. My uncle Tony wasn't a man to waste words. In fact, you'd think they were golden turds the way he held onto them."

The silence deepened as some eyebrows rose incredulously. A few smiles and several nods let Billy know he was understood. He went on.

"A lot of you may not know that Tony wasn't actually deaf up until the last couple of years. To be blunt, he just didn't find most of what you said interesting enough to pay attention to." He scanned the audience and found several chagrined faces, heard a few sympathetic chuckles.

"I trolled with Tony when I was in high school and through the first few years of college. I came home after my freshman year so full of words I couldn't hold them all in. Big words. I went on for hours about existentialism and socialism, nihilism and expressionism and impressionism, communism, cubism...Tony, he didn't say much. He just nodded his head now and then and sometimes he'd say, 'Yup' or 'Nope' or 'Could be'.

"Next morning when I got up he was just putting his dishes away and I asked, 'What's for breakfast?' And he says over his shoulder as he's going out the door, 'Well now, I had ham and eggs, but if you was to look around you might be able to find some 'isms' to fill your belly.'"

The crowd laughed openly and nodded in unison.

"Of course, there never was an 'ism' could fill anybody's belly or his family's bellies either. Tony knew that. He once said to me he thought most politicians were a waste of perfectly good oxygen and most college professors had been educated out of any common sense they once had. So, in deference to Tony, to a life well lived, a family well loved, and principles well served, I'll shut up now and save oxygen for others who have words, big or small, to say about Tony."

The old maple floor creaked comfortingly as he walked, head bowed, to his chair.

Syd rose, shook his hand as they passed, and walked to the mike. Ever the master storyteller, he gave his audience a slow and thorough evaluation before clearing his throat.

"Tony always did feel cemeteries were a bad waste of good real estate, so tomorrow, his ashes will be scattered along his favorite--and secret--king salmon drag. And if you think I'm going to tell you where that is," he added with mock menace, "forget it!"

Chuckles rose as heads either nodded in understanding or shook in wondered appreciation.

"Except for secret fishing holes, Tony was the most generous man I ever met. He first came to Alaska between the world wars by way of Canada and did the Norski hopscotch across Minnesota and the Dakotas, tarried a few years in Ballard before settling here. He crewed on all the great boats, the *Arne*, the *Skaffelstad*, the *Norby*, the *Pelican*. He was a good hand and a good friend. My uncle Walt was on board the *Pelican* with him one year and got caught in the bight of a setting line. It pulled him over the rail before he knew what was happening. Tony reached over the rail, grabbed him by the scruff of the neck, nipped the line in two and set him back on deck. Walt never even got wet.

'You want to watch your feet there, little fella,' was all Tony said. Bear in mind that my uncle weighed over 200 pounds and Tony never broke 160 soaking wet. Walt still doesn't know how Tony did it."

Heads nodded. Smiles quavered. Eyes were dabbed. Syd continued. "After Tony got his own rig, he broke in many of the next generation of fishermen. Let's just see how many of us spent a season or more apprenticed under him."

Necks craned and chairs squeaked as one arm after another rose from the sea of Norwegian sweaters and dark suits.

"I'd say that's close to a third of us," nodded Syd. His full gray beard bobbed up and down on his chest. "I never fished for him, but I fished beside him many years and he always played by the rules. And he expected you to play by the rules, too. One day a big fiberglass rig from outside showed up on his grounds. They traded passes port to port all morning long until this fella thought he'd help himself to Tony's turn. Tony moved out of his way into a big circle, lowered his anchor a few fathoms and came in right behind this fella's stern." Syd made a broad sweeping motion with one arm then turned the hand of it into a scissors. "Snagged all four lines off that big rig faster than you could say 'Fair is fair'. That fella pulled what was left of his gear and steamed off. We never saw him again. But at the end of the season, Tony looked up his address and sent him all his gear coiled up in a cardboard box."

Syd nodded slowly again as his bushy eyebrows swept the room. "Yes, Tony believed fair was fair. So, he sent that fella back his gear, but he sent it postage collect."

Laughter exploded into bunched handkerchiefs. Syd slid his hands into the pockets of his trousers exposing bright red suspenders under his suit jacket. He rocked on his heels, looked up at the high ceiling, and added, "Tony, wherever you are, I wish you fair weather and heavy fishing. You were a good friend."

Before Syd reached his seat, Ed Lovejoy rose in the back of the room. He made his way slowly to the front escorted by swiveling heads. Ed wore the somber suit as though he'd been born into it. Years behind the desk at the bank had shaped him to fit its confines. He bent his tall frame to bring his mouth closer to the microphone.

"Tony..." he leaned back surprised to hear himself bouncing back from the paneled walls. He eased forward again and spoke barely above a whisper.

"Tony did his business at the bank about once a year. He trusted the cannery to keep his accounts and trusted us to make his payments on time. But when he did come in, he'd amble into my office and sit down. We didn't shoot the breeze, as you can imagine. We didn't talk about the fishing or the missus or the kids. When Tony sat down he'd give me a hand written list of fishermen and crewmen he was willing to back if they came to me for a loan. Those lists included pretty much everyone in this room at one time or another."

Ed's long neck carried his head around to eye the audience, wall to wall, and back to the microphone. "A few times—very few times—bad luck struck, payments got late, people on those lists came to me to arrange loans or extensions of one kind or another. I was always able to do that, because I knew Tony would make good if they didn't. He never once had to, of course, and of course, what he was really doing was teaching me to have more faith in the people of this town than stone cold numbers or my banker's instincts told me to. He taught me about the basic goodness in people. And..." He stopped to still the wobble in his voice, blinked at the steely sky outside the narrow windows. "...and there was nobody in this town better equipped to teach that than Tony."

If Ed had more to say it was lost in the folds of numerous handkerchiefs. Pulling his own neatly pressed square of white from his breast pocket, he dabbed at his eyes as he made his way back to his seat.

Dwayne Dickson, who had been leaning against the side wall, pushed himself to a stand. Arms still folded across his chest, he cleared his throat and waited for heads to find him. Without the aid of the microphone, his voice filled the hall.

"Now I don't want you all to go away from here thinking Tony was some kind of saint. We fished together for a lot of years and I saw many sides Tony. He woulda done anything for you, especially if you were in trouble. But he's also the one thought we should plant some grizzlies here on the island. Thought it would go a long way toward improving the deer population by knocking out the wolves and the black bear plus he figured it would keep the pesky tourist population down. Sure, a few of us might complain about getting mauled on the way to the post office, but he figured it'd be worth it to get rid of the outlanders."

More than a few listeners chuckled gratefully and nodded recalling Tony's impatience with what he called freaks and foreigners.

"Tony was working on some deck machinery one real wet summer day. Standing there like a mad heron, rain pouring down the back of his neck and dripping off the end of his nose. This woman comes by all gussied up like a page out of Eddie Bauer, Goretex and poly-who-knows-what, carrying a cute little umbrella and she starts going on and on about the terrible weather. Didn't the sun ever shine here? Don't you get tired of the rain? Was this as warm as it got in the summer? Tony turns his head toward her real slow and says, 'Weather was fine until you showed up.'"

Everyone laughed recalling the familiar look they had all seen on Tony's face and the one they could only imagine on the face of the tourist.

"I do believe she left town inside of ten minutes. And damned if ten minutes later, the sun didn't come out and it stayed out for a month!"

Tony's friends laughed easily, comfortably.

"And Tony loved to hunt and trap. He wasn't gung ho about killing things and never wasted anything he could find a use for. He hunted to put food on the table and trapped to put money in the bank. And I know it's true what Billy said about there being nothing wrong with Tony's hearing.

One day I tramped all over creation and saw nothing. Come out on the beach dog tired just at dark and there sits Tony with two big bucks. So I asks him where'd he see them since I hadn't seen so much as a track. 'Didn't see 'em,' he says, 'Heard 'em. Heard this one taking a leak and heard this one take a dump.' 'How'd you know it wasn't me out there in the brush?' I asks him, 'How'd you know you weren't shootin' at me?' He looks me up and down real slow and says, 'Ain't neither one of 'em said, 'Aaahhh!'

"He didn't miss much," said Dwayne when the crowd had gone quiet again, "but he will be much missed." He leaned back against the wall and brushed two small tears from his own eyes.

As no one could top the Aaahhh story and what needed to be said had been said, the piano struck up the traditional Norwegian tune about 'On the Deck I Stand at Night' and everyone sang some pure or pidgin version of it. Billy went to the microphone again.

"On behalf of the family, I want to thank you all for coming. As Syd said, at Tony's request his ashes will be spread along his favorite fishing drag, so there will be no service at the cemetery. Tony did have one request of all of you though. He did ask that everyone who didn't hold against it should drink to him and to each other. Please join us in celebrating Tony's life."

He raised his hand toward the back where trays and trays of meats, sandwiches, cheeses, and desserts were appearing. The bar was rolled

179

out along the side and the gathering broke into small groups that laughed and hugged and told stories they hadn't had the courage to send out over the microphone.

Jim gave Carla's shoulders a squeeze and slipped away to get them drinks. Carla watched him go. No one could top him in a suit, she thought, shoulders like a barn door and hips like a high schooler. Wait till I get him home, she smiled to herself.

Her Aunt Myra appeared at her side. "So embarrassing," she was saying.

"What?" asked Carla through a hug, "the deer story? Oh, Myra, I don't think so. Everyone's heard it at least once. It was just right." Her eyes strayed back to the direction Jim had taken.

"I just don't think it was the time or the place."

"Don't worry about it. Now's not the time to try to make Tony into something he wasn't."

"Still, I feel like I should go apologize to his girls. Do you think I should?"

Carla found Tony's daughters, gray haired and ample, near the front. They were dabbing eyes, giving and receiving consolation.

"They look fine to me, but if it will make you feel better, go ahead."

"Oh, I don't know. I don't want to make it into something bigger than it already is."

"Why don't you sit down and think about it—or don't think about it. Jim will be back in a second with something to drink."

She found him again in the crowd and when she did both hands balled into fists and slid protectively over her stomach. Jim's long arms were wrapped around a willowy redhead, fondling her back, his face buried in her neck. When he pulled back nodding and flashing that killer grin, she recognized Sara, Billy's daughter, Tony's grandniece, whom she hadn't seen in at least 10 years and who owed her considerably more loyalty than this.

In the crowd near Jim she saw sidelong looks of envy on the men's faces and saw the women nearby craning necks with studied casualness, searching the room for her. She sat down hard and stared at the broad navy blue back of Sigurd Munsen.

She shook her head and blinked the sting away. It was she who had taken Sara under her wing after Billy's divorce, had taught her how to defend herself against cranky outboards and hormone crazed boys, had taken her camping, had helped her buy her first bra, had shown her how to clean a fish and how to put on make up. They had practically been sisters, inseparable for a time. She thought Sara was a friend even if Jim was not.

"Doesn't Evelyn look well?" said Myra. "They had to do a complete you know what."

"No, what?" mumbled Carla absently.

"You know, they had to take out absolutely everything."

Carla focused sharply on her aunt. "A hysterectomy isn't everything, Myra. At least they left her her dignity."

It was Myra's turn to look confused.

"Excuse me," said Carla and she stood slowly as if unsure that the old wooden floor would hold together. Wordlessly she wove to the rear of the hall, skirting knots of chatter and ignoring the sound of her own name. She found her coat, left the hall and let the heavy doors slam behind her. Her heels rang hollowly on the old boardwalk, echoing the hollowness in her bones.

"Can't do it," she thought, "I just can't do it."

A mist began to settle on her hair and a clamminess crept inside her coat.

"I can't do it," she repeated.

She heard running steps behind her. Jim's, but she didn't slow or turn.

"Carla," he called, "what now, for Chrissake?"

"I can't do it," she said, "I saw you. I saw you and Sara and I just can't live like this anymore."

He had caught her up now and pulled her around to face him. She did not resist but stood with tears coursing down her cheeks.

"Saw what? Saw me promise to get Sara a copy of the picture we have of you two painting Tony's boat? Is that what you saw?"

"I don't know. I don't know what you were planning. I just know I can't stand it anymore."

He took a long breath and exhaled slowly. "Think about this. Think about what you're throwing away. All of you means you trust me, Carla. All of me means you can trust me. Think about this."

"I can't." She shook her head hopelessly. "I can't."

"You can, but you won't." His eyes were two naked bulbs burning in a dead end street. "I thought you had more balls than that."

"I think maybe I did...once." Her jaw was set hard, but her eyes soft as they flicked over his face as if to memorize each plane and pore. When he reached for her hand, she took a step backward, then another.

"Good bye," she said simply and turned away. Unable to lift her eyes from the planks below her uncertain feet, she began to walk. Both hands crept up and flattened at the base of her throat. She gulped tiny mouthfuls of air, but breath would not enter her chest, for it crawled with hungry animals gnawing at the ragged remains of her heart. Cold company, she knew, but company she would always be able to count on.

Earl slowed when he saw Betty walk out of the hardware store. She was busy tearing the plastic off of a package of seat covers and didn't see him behind her. Now that Neil Esterhaus was gone, Earl thought maybe they could talk this thing out. He squared his shoulders, stepped manfully forward, then stumbled to a puzzled halt behind her.

He watched, mouth agape, as she marched right up to Belle's Buick and opened the door like she owned the thing. She leaned inside and fitted the elastic around the driver's seat. His curiosity drew him to the curb.

"What are you doing?" he asked incredulous.

"Oh. There you are." She tossed him the other cover. "You gotta hook the elastic around the frame. Be sure you pull it tight."

"What are you doing?" he repeated as he stretched the cover over the passenger seat.

"What's it look like I'm doing? I'm putting seat covers in my car."

"Your car?"

"My car. I bought it from Belle."

"With what?" he demanded.

"With the profit we're going to make fishing my IFQs this year. Actually, only part of it. I haven't decided yet what to do with the rest."

"But we haven't fished that poundage yet."

"But we're going to, aren't we? And when we do," she said with careful deliberation, "every year when we do, I decide where that money goes."

They stared at each other through the open car, fists on the seats and behinds in the street and on the sidewalk respectively. Earl was the first to blink. In his relief at hearing 'we, we, we, and we' all he could think to say was, "So you bought a car with worn out seats?"

"No, Earl, the seats are perfect and I want them to stay that way. Get in. I'll drive you home."

Earl pulled the vise grips and the needle nosed pliers from his back pocket before sliding into the seat. He pulled the door closed and smiled at the heavy reassuring thunk.

Betty signaled and pulled out onto Main Street. She and the engine purred contentedly. Earl reached for the radio then stopped himself.

"May I?" he asked.

"Sure," she said.

He found the power button and pressed it on. The last strains of 'Stars and Stripes Forever' filled the car from four powerful speakers.

"Well, ain't that something!" grinned Earl.

"Turn it down a little, would you?"

He did just as Harold cued his microphone.

"Well, folks, it's been a Count Your Blessings kind of week. What with two near drownings, a daring rescue, the peaceful passing of an old friend, and, from what Emily tells me, a proposal of marriage, the old burg has really been buzzing.

But more shocking than all of that is the miraculous conversion that took place in the editorial page this week. Let me just read this to you," he said, an unmistakable smile creeping into his voice.

"'It is high time government was reminded that it was instituted to serve the governed and not the other way around. What we need is fewer regulations and more service, less meddling and more compassion...' Now doesn't that sound to you like Editor Pinkstad is knocking at the door, begging for admission to the human race? My, my. There may be hope for the old boy yet."

Harold could be heard refolding the newspaper and when he next spoke he had leaned close to the mike. His voice was low and confidential.

"By the way, Arlen, 'of the people, by the people, for the people'? It's been done."

Several seconds of dead air drove the knife home.

"Well, now, I've got a special song here by Nat King Cole ready to go, but first, what do you say we have a look at the Birthday Book for this week? Sunday, May 9th, Helena Esterhaus has a birthday. Happy birthday, Helena. May 10th, Marilyn Olsen and her daughter, Patience, both have birthdays. Patience. Now isn't that a beautiful name? I wonder why more people don't use descriptive names like that. Sort of like the Seven Dwarfs did or the Indians. It must have been a lot more entertaining when people had names like Nose-in-the-Air, Dog's Breath, Carbuncle Face. I wonder what my name would have been. I know! Everyone call in with your own suggestion. Keep it clean now and we'll dig up a prize for the best name, somebody's dirty old coffee mug or last year's calendar. We'll come up with something and we'll announce the winner next week. Put your thinking caps on, Nimblewits. Everyone is eligible except Emily. I've already heard a dozen unkind suggestions from her.

"So anyway, where was I? Ah yes, May 11th, no birthdays, but...uh oh. Emily, this says it's Earl and Betty Dahlberg's wedding anniversary. What's the status?"

"Harold, why don't you just let the Dahlbergs worry about that? Read the dang weather, would you?"

"The weather. As you wish, my queen."